DEMONS

John Shirley

DEMONS

John Shirley

CEMETERY DANCE PUBLICATIONS

Baltimore
❖ 2000 ❖

Signed Hardcover Edition ISBN1-58767-002-X

DEMONS Copyright © 2000 by John Shirley

Dustjacket Design Copyright © 2000 by Gail Cross

Artwork Copyright © 2000 by Erik Wilson

Novella Series
Book 9

FIRST EDITION

Cemetery Dance Publications
P.O. Box 943
Abingdon, Maryland 21009
www.cemeterydance.com

For Richard Smoley

LEXICON
List of Demon clans (vernacular nick-names)

TAILPIPES — Massive, Leviathans, but varying in shape, at will; often more or less like a giant slugshape—nothing like a head on it. Skin may erupt with mouths, which steam. Show no sentience—may be controlled or dominated by Gnashers

SPIDERS — Four-legged but spiderish in shape; intelligent yet arachnoid/insectile in activity—airborne via skygliding 'chutes of web

SHARKADIANS — airborne with rows of smallish leather wings that shouldn't be big enough to carry it but do—head is *all jaws*—body ostensibly like a human female; clawed hands and feet. Pure savagery. May be dominated by Bugsy's.

DISH-RAGS — shaped like bunches of furry rags big as VWs; can contort so they resemble some sea creature—no definite shape —wraps and slowly crushes—often accompanied by psychic/ metaphysical/quantum continuum disruption...

GNASHERS — talkative, at times, appear to have an agenda, verbal sadism, telepathic, humanish but four-armed, jaws like Sharkadians though the mouth parts are a little smaller, and with the addition of upper head parts, human eyes—possibly function in a leadership capacity but no one is quite certain

GRINDUMS — giant grasshopper legs, insectile/human heads, curling horns, big grinding jaws that move sideways, or at an angle, or revolve, as they choose—jaws can turn on their skulls like an owl's head on its shoulders—can generate great heat at will

BUGSYS — parodies of human, no two alike but all in similar style, complete with skin that resembles clothing, but spotted with oozing sores... can sometimes be stymied for awhile by offering to play cards with them—they love gambling...Tend to chatter idiotically...Like the Gnashers speak English or any language of Earth at will—or their own tongue.

Demon Language: Tartaran

Who is a holy person? The one who is
aware of others' suffering.

—Kabir

a prologue

It's amazing what you can get used to. That was a platitude; now it summarizes life for everyone. It means something powerful now. People can get used to terrible privation; to famine, to war, to vast and soulless discount stores. They got used to prison; some got used to living alone on mountain-tops. But now...

This morning I saw a man, a choleric looking, pop-eyed sort of a middle-aged man, in a threadbare suit, stop his huffing old Volvo at a street corner, look about for cross traffic, accelerate slowly to creep across the intersection— the traffic lights, of course, not having worked for a long time, not through the whole north of the state—and then one of the Demons turned the street to soft hot tar as it rose up howling from the stuff of the street itself, rows of fangs in the creature's absurdly big jaws gleaming and dripping. The demon was one of the Grindum clan—giant grasshopper legs, insectile heads with just enough human about them to sicken; curling horns, big grinding jaws that move sideways, or at an angle, or revolve, turn on their skulls like an owl's head on its shoulders; the Grindum was swimming in the hot asphalt with a conventional freestroke; humming some tune as it swam.

The Volvo began to sink in the steaming, tarry asphalt. The Volvo driver merely got a good grip on his briefcase, opened the car door, used the door handle for a ladder rung, ran along the roof of the car to the hood, and jumped from the Volvo to the curb. Landing rather neatly, he continued on his way, not even looking back, hurrying only a little. The commuter didn't even turn around as the demon, chattering in Tartaran, snapped the door off the car, and sailed it through the window of a bank. The bank was long closed, as most of them are now.

A woman came out of a bar, too drunk to heed the warnings of her friends, and the demon heaved the car atop her, his iridescent, green-black, scaly torso still halfway sunken into the tarry street. I wondered absently if he were standing on a pipe down there, under the street.

I had already turned away from the street corner, and saw all this glancing over my shoulder, now and then, in a measured retreat. If you ran in panic, the demon was more likely to notice you, and pursue, especially the Grindum clan. The Sharkadians, on the other hand, are more methodical, and when they've selected a neighborhood they'll stalk through it, and cut you down as they find you, (or toy with you and leave you sorrowfully alive, wishing they'd killed you), whether you're running or not.

I made it around the corner. I heard another scream but didn't go back to look. I had an appointment to teach art to children, and was looking forward to it. Creating little personal works of art raises them, for a few minutes, out of the fear and depression that haunts the young now, though the art usually expresses fear of the demons. And when they're raised up a little, in that moment of self expression, they raise me up with them.

So I was not going to risk being late for the session. Or risk, for that matter, being torn limb from limb, or sat upon and whispered to for hours before being dispatched. My heart was beating faster, as I hurried away, but I was all right. I was...

Used to it? I suppose it isn't really true. You can't be *really* used to them. You can only adapt, more or less.

But not everyone has. Certainly more people than ever before go quite mad, utterly psychotic, on a daily basis; driven mad by the presence of hundreds of thousands of flesh and blood demons who appear randomly and all too frequently among us now. Those who were mad before the transfiguration of the world feel more at home.

Some of those who were the babbling neighborhood schizophrenics sport a rather annoying look of smug vindication, these days.

People sometimes tell jokes about the demons. "How can you tell a Sharkadian from a Gnasher?"

"Easy—a Gnasher doesn't like a screwtop cap—he always uses real cork to stop up their necks after he pulls their heads off." (You had to be there. A Gnasher has the reputation of being a snob. They put on aristocratic airs.)

For a brief while, some said it was all a hoax; in the first day or two of the demonic invasion you could dismiss even the television footage as staged, perhaps special effects, a government scam to necessitate martial law. Often those who made such a claim in the media met a demon within minutes; they were then reduced, in the butcher's sense of the term, or watched their loved ones reduced.

There are some who said, for a time, that the coming of the Seven Clans of demons to the world—their random dominance of the world, in daylight as much as night and without need for summoning magicians—was a fulfillment of prophecy. If the commentator was Christian they said it fulfilled Revelations; the Jews and the Sikhs and Muslims pointed to other prophecies. The fundamentalist Christians, anyway, were easily refuted: the Second Coming part never came about. They waited and waited for the Judgment; for the angel with the flaming sword, for the Rapture, for the dead to rise (now and then the demons raise the dead, but not the way the Christians expected), for Jesus to come in his glory.

Jesus was a no-show. Naturally, the evangelists rationalize his conspicuous absence: the Sacred Timetable, don't you know, is a little off, that's all. But the most 'righteous' of them are eaten alive, a limb at a time, in public, no differently than 'sinners'. I remember when the demons rampaged through Oral Roberts University. The sniggering delight that some hipsters and cynics took in this brutal series of bloody atrocities was most embarrassing—for the rest of us cynics and hipsters.

People adapt; they have their little ways. Some adapt by giving the demons little classification nicknames, names like "Gnashers" and "Dishrags" somehow making the creatures seem less threatening; or by spinning theories about them, trying to evolve methods of avoiding or controlling them, none of which work. There were TV specials for a while, demands on Congress, the short lived National Guard assaults, resulting in forty thousand dead soldiers. The TV series: the World in Crisis came to a grinding halt when every reporter was slowly and lovingly masticated by giant Grindums—Clan Four.

There were those, oh of course, who asserted, at first, that the demons were space aliens, or the confabulations of aliens, or multiple races of space aliens come to invade. That the invaders resembled demons only because our past encounters with the aliens left ancestral memories of their shapes, extraterrestrial shapes: remembered as "demons". You know the sort of thing. But anyone who has survived an encounter with one of the seven clans is left with no doubt that these are supernatural creatures; there's no question that they are *quite specifically demonic.* That not only are they not aliens: they distinctly belong here. How does one know this? It's another one of those intangibles that, ironically, define the creatures. Once you've encountered them—you simply know. You can *feel* their miraculous nature; you can feel they're somehow rooted in our world. And after themselves having such encounters, Close Encounters of the Nearly Fatal Kind, the purveyors of ET explanations fall silent.

I'm writing this now because of Professor Paymenz' theory. I should say one of his theories—he has so many. This one is something like Paymenz Theory Number 1,347. Dr. Israel Paymenz believes that we can communicate to other times, other eras, through the medium of a sort of higher, ubiquitous ancestral mind that links all humanity. He believes that writers and poets and declaimers in the past sometimes 'dictate' to writers of the later eras, through this psychic link; that historians of the future communicate, unconsciously and with only partial accuracy, with the writers of the past: thus the more believable science-fiction. So it is that much writing is, unknown to us, a kind of ouija affair; only, the receiver is not hearing from the dead, but from people of another time; from the living of the past and future.

Not very likely, that theory; I doubt he believes it either. But writing this, at a time when I feel resoundingly helpless, makes me feel better.

So I try to believe his theory...which leaves me writing this just eleven years into the 21st century, hoping to warn the previous century, or even earlier. Not warn them of some specific act, or mistake. We don't yet know *why* the seven clans came. But I dream of warning that they will come. So that, perhaps, the people of the past can begin looking for the *why* in advance. The demons certainly have given us no whys, nor hows, nor wherefores. They delight in communicating only what confuses.

Though the demons will talk to us sometimes, they are, of course, notoriously unhelpful. When the President went with a delegation, including the vice president, to see an apparent demon-clan chieftain (we don't know for certain he was a chieftain; their hierarchy is arcane, if they have any at all), who was stalking the west wing of the White house, they had a rather extensive conversation, nearly 15 minutes, which was recorded and analyzed and which offers exchanges like this, transcribed from near its end:

The President: "And why is it, please, that you have come to…to us, now?"

Gnasher chieftain: "Home is where the heart is. Boy Scouts have a salty sort of taste, with marshmallow overtones. I like your tie. Are those Gucci loafers?"

The President: "Yes, yes they are. So you're familiar with all our customs?"

Gnasher: "I've never killed a customs agent. Are they good to kill? Never mind. Where is your wife?"

President: "My…she's…in Florida."

Gnasher: "Does the vice president have sex with her? Which vices does he preside over? I'm just fucking with you about that. But seriously: do you like sweet or salt best?"

President: "Could you tell me please why you have come here and if there's something we can give you…Some arrangement we can make…"

Gnasher: "I wonder what you'd look like inside-out. Like a Christmas tree?"

President: "We are willing to negotiate."

Gnasher: "I can almost taste you now. You once had a dream you cracked open the moon like an egg, and a red yolk came out and you fried it on the burning Earth, didn't you, once, eh? Did you? Do speak plainly, and tell me: did you?"

President: "I don't believe so."

Gnasher: "You did. You dreamt exactly that. People think someone like me would delight in the carnage of a battlefield, but I prefer a nice mall, don't you?"

President: "Yes, certainly. Perhaps in that spirit..."

Gnasher: "You wish to sell me cufflinks? Can you breathe in a cloud of iron filings? Let's find out. Let's discover a new jigsaw, a new three-dee puzzle, shall we? The human body, disassembled, might be put back together in a way that makes sense, you could make a fine Bucky ball out of the bones, and a yurt from the skin, and a talk show host of the wet parts. What an imaginative people you are. We stand in awe of the outskirts of Buenos Aires in the summer time; each fly a musical note. Can we send out for ice cream? For girls who work in ice cream parlors and their boyfriends in their electric TransAms? Taste this part of my leg. It tastes differently from this part. You won't taste? I have a penis. Would you prefer it? Do you like salty or sweet? Seriously. Choose one. Would you like to see my penis? I asked for it special. There's a catalog."

With that, a steaming green member pressed from a fold on the Gnasher's lower parts and as the President tried to back away it caught him in a long ropy sweep of its arm and pulled him close and forced him to his knees. In front of the TV cameras.

An eruption of gunshots from the Secret Service had no effect, of course, on the Gnasher. It was the Vice President —a decisive man, who'd been broodingly biding his time for two years—who took a pistol from the President's bodyguard and shot the President in the back of the head with it. It was obvious to everyone there, and to a sympathetic Congress, the next day, that the Gnasher, after all, was choking the President to death with his engorged steaming green penis. It was a question of restoring dignity to the President, and the office. The Vice President fled the scene, sacrificing a number of Secret Service men whom he ordered to delay the pursuing demon, while he escaped.

"It's profoundly tragic," the vice president said afterwards, "but it's God's will. We must move on. I have certain announcements to make..." He is reported more or less safe in certain underground bunkers.

But I should tell you how it began. It was months ago. Despite the usual outbreaks of savagery, the wet snow of the ordinary was blanketing the world. The miraculous rarely shows itself. When it does, it comes seamlessly, and for some reason, everyone is surprised.

1

As for me…

I was up in a high rise, in San Francisco, those months ago: the morning the demons came.

I had gone up to see Professor Paymenz, or, to be perfectly honest, to see his daughter under the auspices of seeing the Professor. It was housing that San Francisco State had arranged for him—they had a program supplying discounted housing to teaching staff—and as I arrived I saw another eviction notice from SFSU on the door. Paymenz had refused to teach comparative religion anymore, would only lecture about extremely obscure occult practices and beliefs, and rarely showed up even for that. He hadn't ever had his tenure settled, so they simply fired him. But he'd refused to leave the university housing, on the simple (but contumacious) grounds, as he explained, that he deserved this subsidization more than the teacher, down the hall, who taught "existential themes in daytime television"…

Vastly bearded, restless-eyed, wearing the grimy alchemist's robe that he used as a nightgown, Paymenz looked over my shoulder, into the hallway behind me. Expecting to see someone back there. He always did that, and he never met my eyes, no matter how earnestly he spoke to me.

He seemed almost happy to see me, as he ushered me in. He even said, "Why, hello, Ira." It was hard to be certain—he rarely troubled with social niceties.

I saw that Professor Shephard was there, small-brim fedora in hand. Shephard seemed poised between staying and going. Maybe that was why Paymenz was happy to see me: it gave him an excuse to get rid of an unwanted visitor.

Shephard was a short, fiftyish bullet-shaped man in an immaculate gray suit, vest, ties that matched the season, a shaved head, eyes the color of aluminum, a perpetual pursed smile, a jutting jaw.

He put his hat on his head, but didn't go. Standing there in the exact middle of the small living room, with his arms by his side, his small feet in shiny black shoes neatly together, Shephard looked out of place in Paymenz' untidy, jumbled apartment. He looked set up and painted like one of those bowling-pin-shaped Russian toys, the sort made of smooth wood, with ever-smaller interior copies. Shephard was an economics professor who believed in "returning economics to philosophy, as it was with our Founding Fathers, and, yes, with Marx"—but his philosophy had something to do with "pragmatic postmodernism". Today his tie was all coppery maple leaves against rusty orange, celebrating autumn.

I knew Shephard from the last conference on Spirituality and Economics he'd put together—he'd hired me to create the poster, with "appropriate imagery" and paid me three times for doing three versions; each version less definite, blander than the one before. At every poster-design discussion, he'd brought up Paymenz. *"I understand you're his good friend, and what is he up to? And his daughter? How is she?"*

The questions always felt like non-sequiturs. Now, recognizing me, he nodded pleasantly. "Ira. How are you?"

"Dr. Shephard," Paymenz said, before I could reply, "thank you for dropping in—I have guests, as you see..."

Shephard's head swiveled on his shoulders like a turret, first at me, then to Paymenz. "Of course. I am sorry to have precipitated myself upon you, as it were; perhaps certain matters are of some urgency. Perhaps not. I only wished to plant the seed of the idea, so to say, that should the conference on Spiritual Philosophy and Economics not come about, this weekend, for any reason, I do wish to stay in touch—very closely in touch. Please feel free to call me." He handed Paymenz a business card and was moving toward the door. He startled me by *not* seeming to move on rollers; he walked as any man his size might. A normal walk seemed odd on him. "I will speak to the board about your housing issue, as promised, one more time. Au revoir!" He opened, passed through, and closed the door with hardly a sound, smooth as smoke through a chimney.

Paymenz irritably tossed the business card onto a lamp table heaped with cards, unopened letters, bills. "That man's arrogance, the way he just shows up unexpectedly...Always as if he has no agenda...Babbling about his conference not going off—when there's no reason it shouldn't...I should never have agreed to go to his antiseptic-yet-strangely-septic conference, if he hadn't offered me a fee...But he knows perfectly well I need the money."

Hoping Paymenz remembered he actually had invited me over for coffee, I looked around for some place to hang my leather jacket. But of course there was no place, really, to put it. The closet was crammed full with clothes no one wore; with junk. The other apartments in the twenty-story high rise were under-decorated minimalist-modern affairs, trying to re-echo the utilitarian airy, curviness that the architects of the building had borrowed from IM Pei or Frank Lloyd Wright. Paymenz, however, had covered the walls in an ethnically disconnected selection of tapestries and carpets, Persian and Chinese and a Southwestern design from Sears. He collected old lava lamps and, though the electricity had been turned off, they churned away, six of them crudely wired into car batteries, with lots of electric tape around half-stripped connections; the lamps sat on the car batteries, and on end tables and mantels, shape-shifting in waxen primary colors. A week previous, it was said, the entire SFSU board of Tenure Review had come out to the university parking lot to find their cars mysteriously inert.

Half a dozen more lava-lamps were broken, used as book ends for the many hundreds of books that took up most of the space that wasn't tapestry. Two candles were burning, and a fading electric lamp. They used a bucket to flush the toilet. But still, Paymenz wouldn't leave the place...Cats darted behind chairs and moved sinuously up and down much-clawed cat-trees. I counted four cats. No, five: They'd taken in a new one. There were bits of breakfast toast in Paymenz's long, shovel-shaped grey and black beard; his eyes, red-rimmed grey under bristling brows, rested on me only for a flicker as he spoke, "Many the auguries this morning, Ira. Would you like to see?"

"You know how I feel about medieval techniques, especially any that involve damp, decaying guts," I said, looking about for Melissa. I was an aficionado of the arcane metaphysical, being the former art director for the now defunct *Visions: the Magazine of Spiritual Life*, but I drew the line at peering into rotting intestines.

"It's fresh pig bladder," he said. "None of that decaying stuff anymore, Melissa made me promise. I suppose the place is rank enough already."

The place wasn't quite rank but it bore a distinct smell: pipe tobacco and cat boxes and cloying middle eastern incense, all vying for dominance.

"I see you have some new lava lamps."

"Yes. Look at this one—a confection of gold-flecked red ooze fighting its way into a feverish primeval swelling. Unconsciously, the designer was thinking of the Philosopher's Stone."

"I don't know if they bothered with a designer for these things after the first one."

"They don't need one, it's true—and that's the point. The lava lamp is proto-society's purely unconscious expression of the primeval ooze on one level, shaping itself into our most remote sea-slime ancestors; on another, the lava lamp is the pleroma, the fundamental stuff that gives birth to the existential condition. Hank down at the head shop tells me he likes to smoke pot and look into his lava lamps, and then he sees girls there, apparently, in all those sinuous lava-bubbling curves—like Moscoso drawings— but it's all quite unconscious...Tabula rasa for the sub-conscious... Freud not utterly discredited after all, if we consider Hank and his lamps..."

Paymenz noticed my attention wandering; my gaze must have drifted to Melissa's bedroom door. "Oh good lord. Typical young person today. Post MTV generation. Internet surfing brain-damage. Attention span of a gnat. Melissa! Come in here, this young man is already weary of pretending he's here to see me! He's *a-quiver* with desire for you!" He clutched his reeking alchemist's robe about himself—Melissa had made it for him, as a mother will make a superman cape for her little boy—and stumped off on his short legs to the kitchen to finish his breakfast. "He's sniffing the air for your pheromones!" he called to her, as he went.

I grimaced; but I was used to the professor's indifference to social insulation of any kind whatsoever.

Melissa came in then, wearing a long black dress, no shoes; a loose, low cut gypsy-type purple blouse; her crooked smile even more to one side of her triangular face than usual, in wry deprecation of her father's vulgarity.

"Shephard is gone?" she asked.

"He is," I said. "Unless he's somehow watching us through his business card. I don't think nanotech is that far along."

"Wouldn't surprise me. He makes my skin contract on my body," she said, locking the front door. "He asked me if he could hear me sing for him sometime! Like to hear my songs, he said. As if."

I was thinking that Shephard had always had an unhealthy interest in her but decided not to remark on it. My own interest in her, I told myself, was…earthy.

She was a few inches taller than me; a big girl with tiny feet; I don't know how she kept from teetering on them. Her forehead was high, this only mildly mitigated by the shiny black bangs; long raven wings of black hair fell straight to her pale, stooped shoulders and coursed round them. Her large green eyes looked at me frankly; they seemed to coruscate. Her chin was just a little slight. Somehow the imperfections in her prettiness were sexy to me. I suspected, after long, covert inspections from various angles through various fabrics, that her right breast turned fractionally to one side while the other pointed straight ahead. Each small white toe of her small white feet had a ring on it, and her ankles jangled with Tibetan bells. She was thirty, and worked in a health food store, and did endless research for her father's never-finished magnum opus, *The Hidden Reality*.

"Come into the kitchen with me," she said, "and help me make tea and toast."

"I couldn't possibly let you take on a big job like that alone."

She stacked up the wheat bread, and I found the old copper teapot and filled it with tap water. As it filled, I said, "I wonder what particular impurities and pollutants this particular tapwater has in it. No doubt some future forensic archaeologist will analyze my body and find the stuff. Like, 'This skeleton shows residues of lead, pesticides, heavy metal contaminants...'"

"...Which perhaps weighted down his consciousness so he became doleful all the time. Great Goddess! Ira, you can't even pour a cup of tea without seeing doom in the offing?"

I listened to her bells jangle as she got the margarine off the cooler-shelf in the kitchen window—the refrigerator didn't work anymore. I washed out some cups. "I see you've painted your toenails silver." I thought of making a joke about how they might be little mirrors allowing me to see up her dress but decided it would come off more puerile than cute. There were times when it was paradoxically almost sophisticated to be puerile, but this wasn't one of them.

"I mean, it must've occurred to you," she was saying, looking through a cluttered drawer for a butterknife, "that this prevailingly negative view of the world could attract negative consequences."

"The butterknife is in that peanut butter jar on top of the refrigerator. My negative view of the world—I would only believe it would attract negative consequences if I were superstitious," I sniffed. I painted on mystical themes, illustrated for magazines about the supernatural, meditated, and prayed— and I was a notorious skeptic. This irritated some believers, others found it refreshing. I was simply convinced that most of what was taken for the supernatural was the

23

product of the imagination. Most but not all. Sufi masters sometimes say that one of the necessary skills for the seeker is the ability to discriminate between superstition working on the imagination and real spiritual contact. "There are plenty of pessimists who are quite successful in life—look at that old geezer who used to be a film maker...he was just in the news, saying that his application to be part of the rejuvenation experiments was turned down because of some old scandal...what's-his-name. Horn rim glasses."

"Woody Allen, I think. But still, overall, Ira...Hand me the bread...overall, people can think themselves into miserable lives."

"I'm not so miserable. I've got work for a month or two ahead, and I'm playing house right now with someone who..." Suddenly I didn't know how to finish saying it. She glanced at me sidelong and I thought I saw her droop her head so that her hair would swing to hide her smile. I'm an idiot, when I try to express anything but bile, I thought. "Anyway," I went on hastily, "the world needs no help from my 'bad vibes' or whatever you call it. The enormity of the suffering in it...Should we use this Red Rose tea or...You don't have English Breakfast or something? Okay, fine, I like Red Rose too...I mean, regarding the world's own 'negative vibes', simply look at the news."

"Oh no, don't do *that*."

"Seriously, Melissa—Over the last decade or so this country has gotten so corrupt. There was a lot of it already but—now we're becoming like Mexico City. I mean, they discovered that a certain pesticide was causing all these birth defects in the Central Valley—there was a big move to get it banned. But if it was banned the agribusiness and chemicals people would lose money on the poison they kept in reserves. Cut their profit margin. So the ban was killed. And everyone forgot all about it and the stuff is still choking the ecology out there and no one gives a damn. Then the corruption thing gets worse and worse—the feds just found out that all this federal aid that was supposed to go to vaccinating and blood-testing ghetto kids was stolen by all these people appointed to give it out. They just raked it off and put it in other accounts—they stole millions intended for these kids...And a lot of the people doing the stealing were the same ethnicity as the poor they were supposed to be helping. It wasn't racism—it was simple corruption. It was greed. It's like life is a big trough and they're all looking for a way to elbow in and get at the slops and nothing else matters."

"Ira...butter these for me."

"Sure. And did you see that thing on PBS about that country in Central America—the bigshots running the country decided that the fast money would come from making it into a waste dump for all these other countries that ran out of room. The entire country is a waste dump! The whole thing, a landfill! The guys who run the country moved to these pristine little islands offshore and the entire rest of the country works in waste dumps—either they work in them, burning and shoving stuff around with big machines, or they pick through them...Literally millions of people picking through a waste dump thousands of miles across..."

"Oh you must be exaggerating. Surely not the whole country. Bring me that blue teapot."

"I'm not exaggerating. The country is *literally* one giant dump—there is no farmland, there are no wetlands, there are no forests, and there are only a few towns left. It's all dump. Barges come from North America, from Mexico, from Brazil...from the neighboring countries...And people will live and die in that dump. Can you imagine? It's like a great festering sore in the epidermis of the planet—and it's not alone. Why, in Asia..."

"Ira?" She touched my arm. Her fingernails alternated silver with black flecks and black with silver flecks. "The sick get better. The world will suffer, and this will make it see what it has done, and it will heal itself. It will."

I guess we both understood, she and I, that it was a sort of script we had together. The tacit script brought me to her, and I'd tell her that the world was in Hell, for this reason or that, and she'd tell me there was hope, that it would some day be all right, and not to give up on life. I guess we both knew that I came to her for a sort of mothering—my own mother had sickened and died when I was fifteen, from the amphetamines her boyfriend shot into her. I guess we both knew that when Melissa said there was hope for the world, that it really meant there was hope for me.

Melissa always plays along. She is all generosity. She doesn't seem to mind.

I wonder if she wouldn't mind if I made love to her.

"There'll be hard times," she was saying, "but the world will heal."

"Maybe," I said. "Maybe so."

She took her hand away. "Would you carry the toast plate? I'll get the tea pot and the cups." Not an allocation of duty made at random: she took the most breakable stuff herself. I was notorious for my clumsiness.

"Sure. I'll get it."

We ate breakfast, Paymenz and his daughter and me, out on the molded balcony. Breakfast of a sort: we consumed a stack of margarine-slick toast and blood-red tea at the tilting glass-topped wrought-iron table on their concrete balcony-deck, overlooking a mist-draped west San Francisco, under a lowering sky; listening to pigeons cooing from

26

the roof, and sirens sighing from the projects, and the thudding rise and fall, like armies passing, of hip-hop boxes booming in the asphalt plaza below.

I watched the pulse of traffic on the boulevard visible between the glassy buildings of the hospital complex. The traffic would pulse one way, then that artery would come to a stop and the cross-hatch direction would pulse by at right angles; then the first artery would resume pumping. Cars and trucks and SUVs and vans; about twenty percent of them were electric now. Was the air cleaner, with the electric cars? Not much—there were so many more people now which meant many more cars of both kinds.

The professor spoke of his wrangles with the University personnel board, his demands for back pay, and repeatedly asked me to look at the bladders and the entrails he had cut open and kept in an ice chest with some of that perma-ice stuff, so that he could scry for us the patterns that would become the future, and I said no, I would be content if Melissa would bring out her Tarot cards, for Tarot cards have no appreciable smell, and he had just said, "Ah but that's where you're wrong." Just then the mist that had been hanging in the air seemed to drift upward over the plaza, and the clouds overhead developed drippy places on their undersides, like the beginnings of tornadoes, but which, instead of giving birth to tornadoes, expanded into thick globules of vitreous emulsion, like drops hanging from the ceiling of a steam sauna, getting heavier and heavier. The birds had fallen silent; the air grew turgid with imminence. Dr. Paymenz and Melissa and I found ourselves as silent as the birds, gazing expectantly out at the clouds, at the city, and then again up at the strangely shaped clouds, now as if the sky had developed nipples that were giving out a strange effluvium; but now the droplets up above bulged, and seemed to swarm within themselves—

2

"Dad?" Melissa said, in a voice that quavered only a little.

He reached out and took her hand but kept watching the sky.

—and then the droplets burst, like fungus pods giving out black spores, and the specks of black took on more definite shape, shapes that soared and dropped, and called from the distance with hooting, anticipatory glee, and then we saw little black cones forming on the streets below, and exuding not volcanism but inverted teardrops, mercuric and quivering, that burst in counterpoint to cloud drops, scattering nodes of black that took shape and joined their fellows from above; and we saw them drifting closer, coming toward us and to the other buildings in the city; growing as they came not only in perspective but in individual size; and one of them—with a row of leather wings, like thistle leaves, up and down its back—came to grip the building, five stories below, with long ropy arms and legs that ended in eagle's claws. It was what we later came to call a Sharkadian: Its body was theoretically female—with leathery green-black breasts and a woman's hips and even a vaginal slit—but gender is only a parody amongst the demons. The Sharkadian's head didn't maintain the mock femininity—it was a set of jaws and only jaws, and it used them to bite off a chunk of concrete balcony. It chewed meditatively for a moment and then spat wet sand. A man came out on the balcony beside it, to see what all the shouting from the street was, and got out half a scream before the Sharkadian leapt on him, and snapped part of his skull away, not quite enough to kill him instantly—it's been noted many times that the creatures rarely dispatch anyone quickly; they always play with their food. In the square below there was deep throated laughter and weeping, pursuit hither-thither; while on the balcony the Professor began to intone, so rapidly he seemed to be thinking hysterically aloud, something like, "It was this morning that I reflected that science knows all and nothing at once; that they may assert that the core of the atom is the nucleus, a hydrogen atom comprising a single stable, positively charged particle, the proton, say; electrons around other sorts of particles making a kind of shell of particle-wave charge, and they are entirely correct, yet all they're doing is labeling phenomena, just labeling, labeling..."

Melissa came to cling to me, but I could not enjoy the contact. I was about to drag her inside, to tentative safety, when a demon—one of the almost elegant Gnashers, clashing its teeth as it came—settled into the balcony beside ours; and then we were petrified, unable to move. We watched as a terrified woman on the neighboring balcony— Mrs. Gurevitz, I think her name was — tried to flee back inside; the demon pulled her close and, typical of the Gnashers, simply forced her to sit down and engaged her in conversation, for a while, telling her unctuously that it saw in her mind that she hated her bullying husband but was afraid to leave him because of the money problem, because she had no skills, and why didn't she have skills, because she was basically a mistake perpetrated by her mother in a careless moment, not a real person who could develop skills, not like her sister, who was a lawyer, *there* was someone real. And the woman writhed in her chair as both the demon and the professor droned on. The Professor saying, *sotto voce*, to no one in particular: "They may assert, for example, that the region in subatomic space in which an electron is mostly likely to be found is called an orbital, but it's just a label, a tag used in describing the behavior of certain forces under certain conditions, that description accurate but offering no real insight into the nature of that thing—they don't know *why* the atom is that way, even if they can describe the series of events that took it there, it's just as mysterious as if they'd never studied it at all…"

I was sure, at the moment, that he'd gone quite mad—or was stunned into a stream-of-consciousness volubility.

Finally, as I saw four demons coming toward us through the air, I began to struggle inwardly with my paralysis, with a rigidity of fear so pronounced that wrenching loose from it seemed to tear something in my mind.

But there—I was moving, I could grab the professor's arm, and Melissa, and pull them toward the glass sliding doors to the kitchen—as the group of four demons drifted closer, closer, these creatures who were appetite personified, whom I'd later know as Spider clan, drifting with their wispy bodies toward us on hang gliders of spun glass that they express from their loins, coming closer and very deliberately to our balcony and no other…

We stumbled through the open doorway, and I pushed the professor and his daughter behind me, and fumblingly slid the glass door shut—I locked it, though the act seemed to mock me with its futility.

3

The spidery things that had drifted to the balcony were not eight legged, like spiders, but only three legged, tripodal, each leg, long and thin and jointed and featherish like certain spiders—but big, each leg about two-and-a-half yards long —and their upper parts, initially only as big as laundry baskets, were like oversized suction cups, with a single yellow eye that seemed to slide around the convex topside at will, slitting the skin as it went to peer out where it would. There was a sucking mouth part in the concave underside, where the three legs met; a membrane on the rim exuded the web stuff, like ectoplasm that mimicked spider silk. The connection to the parachute of demonsilk broke when it latched onto the balcony, and its sail drifted and fell and turned to the ground far below— where cars were exploding and fires gushing up— like a flag cut from a pole.

The three legged spider thing sucked itself closer to the balcony, one of its legs probing at the doorway...

I pushed the still-babbling professor to the hall door—started to open it, and then fell silent—listening to the bubbling, breathing sound from the other side. From the hall. The low chuckle. The whimper. Someone's "Please... please don't..." suddenly cut off. "Ple—"

I put the door-chain in place. Paymenz had his arms around Melissa, whose face had gone so gray I was afraid for her.

Paymenz' expression changed from second to second; one moment delighted wonder, then sorrow, then fear—fear for Melissa, as he looked at her.

I stepped into the doorway to the kitchen and peered around the edge of the dead refrigerator—which Melissa filled with racks of dirt and used to grow salad mushrooms. I peered at the glass doors, expecting to see them shattering. But instead, the tremulous creatures seemed to have settled down onto the balcony, draping themselves over it, extending their legs to grip the outer walls, the outdoor light fixture, the drain pipe, the doorframe, arranging themselves at odd angles to one another; they seemed to be in a languid state of waiting. Then someone was drawn up, thrashing, from below, snatched perhaps from a lower balcony: a Chinese gentleman, in a powder-blue suit. Perhaps he was from the Asian Studies department—the thought echoing in my head, ludicrously irrelevant. Round face quivering with terror, arms pinioned to his sides by the demonsilk that wound around him, he was hoisted by the silk to the Spider Clan demons. The two nearest him pulled him apart between them, with swift movements of their giant-pipecleaner legs, and stuffed him into their suctioning maws; their bodies expanded to encompass the gushing halves of him, and then rippled, squeezing and relaxing, squeezing and relaxing, pulping him inside. He lived long enough for a brief muffled scream. Then they spat out the empty skins like grape peels.

A moment later the demon who'd had the upper half of the Chinese gent began to convulse, to shudder—then to strain like a woman in birth, to exude, from its nether membranes, a finer ectoplasm that spun to form itself into shapes...Shapes of Chinese children, a Chinese woman, a ghostly boy...

Members of the man's family? His memory of himself?

The other spider toyed with these productions as they emerged, pulling them apart, sniffing at them with the ends of their legs where I saw something like nostrils near the grasping claws...

Then I felt the professor pull me back into the living room. He seemed to be swaying, in front of me, far away and yet very near. But it was I who was swaying.

"You were about to faint, young man," he said. "Your knees were buckling."

"Yes." After a moment, sinking onto the edge of a sofa's arm, I said, "It's not a dream, is it?"

"No."

"What do we do now?"

Paymenz sighed. He sat down heavily on a split-open ottoman. "First—I apologize. I...began to babble out there. I was useless. Useless as...as bosoms on a...whatever that expression is. That's always been my failure—faced with the abyss—which, really, is just an infinity of possibilities— I crumble. Into drink, sometimes. And Good Lord I need a drink...But as for what to do—this calls for, ah, emergency measures. And we must have...we must obtain...information—so we must do the unthinkable. Melissa..." He took a deep breath, and then he made the decision, and he spoke it aloud: *"Take the television out of the closet...and turn it on!"*

He said this the way another man would say, "Get the shotguns out, and load them."

To Paymenz, a television was more dangerous than a shotgun.

"The phenomenon seems to be global," the newscaster was saying. "And it seems to be genuine. Early reports of mass hallucinatory drugs introduced into the water system, and an outbreak of rye-mold toxicity, turn out to be wrong—as we here at KTLU can attest. Our own Brian Smarman was brutally killed this afternoon by the phenomenon." He was an almost cardboard cut-out news-caster; his hair looked like it had been poured into a cast, and, like many local newscasters, he was heavily caked in makeup. His voice quavered only a little.

"Did you ever notice," I said hoarsely, "that the closer you get to Los Angeles, where the anchormen want to be, the better looking they are; we're halfway up the state from Los Angeles so we get the offbrand-looking newscasters. Up around Redding they're all goofy-looking ducks who're saving their money to buy condos..."

"Have *you* ever noticed," Melissa interrupted, gesturing for me to be quiet, "how you tend to toss out irrelevant remarks when you're nervous?"

I had noticed it, actually, yes.

The newscaster was going on hesitantly. "We..." He looked at the paper, seemed to misdoubt if he should read it, and went on, "We are calling it 'the phenomenon' because there is such disagreement about the nature of the attacks. Alien invasion, invaders from another dimension, robots created by an enemy nation, and the first signs of...of Judgment Day—we've heard all these explanations... Observers from the station here..." His voice broke a little. "...seem to agree that...that the beings in question are demonic, or supernatural. However an anthropologist who encountered the beings and lived—I do not seem to have his name here—believes that they could be 'some other form of biological life...'"

"Now will scholarship's imbeciles have their day," Professor Paymenz muttered.

"Shh, Dad," Melissa chided him. She held onto his arm. We were all three of us huddled on her bed, in her bedroom, the farthest from the hall and the porch; the little satellite-seeker TV plugged in on her bed. How I'd longed, in better times, to be in her bed.

"...Oh we have a brief interview with a...it just says a 'theorist from San Francisco State'...Dr. Laertes Shephard..."

"Shephard!" Paymenz burst out. "A theorist is he! Why don't they mention why he's here instead of at Stanford—kicked out of Stanford..."

Footage of Shephard looking strangely calm and collected, standing by a window, smoke rising from the skyline beside him. "...We will need to look at this phenomenon from every angle, from fresh angles, from below if necessary, as it were, and ask ourselves, could this be a part of the natural order, just coming into its own? Perhaps this is not their first time here—could they have visited Earth at the time of the dinosaurs and contended with the great reptilians? Could they come along to precipitate a jump in evolution? If we understand their natural function we will..."

"We lost that feed," the newscaster muttered, as he replaced Shephard. "We..." He seemed to stare into space for a moment.

"Poor man," Melissa said, looking at the newscaster. "He so wants to run and hide."

"Why did they interview Shephard?" I asked. "What's an economist got to do with all this?"

"Putting a finger in every intellectual pie is his specialty," Paymenz growled. "He insists that economics is natural selection and natural selection is economics, got a minor degree in biology so he could make the argument and not be laughed at…"

"We…we'll go on now to…" The newscaster was shuffling through the paperwork on his desk as if it was something that newscasters actually used. "I have here somewhere…" The newscaster looked off-camera. His lower lip quivered. A shadow fell over him. He lunged from his seat, leaving the shot, and the image dissolved into snow.

But the sound feed continued for a moment. "They—!" It sounded like the same newscaster but his voice was attenuated by distance and terror. "—demons, just—my family—if you could—stay in your—*No!*"

Then came a voice, speaking in some language I didn't recognize. A silky voice, but the silk ribbon stretched into an infinity of darkness.

The professor dived the length of the bed, nearly bouncing the little TV off as he went, stabbing at the button on the built-in digital recorder.

"Dad—we *do* have a remote!" Melissa said.

"Quiet, girl…"

A voice babbled from the static and snow in some unknown language. It rose and fell in painfully unfamiliar accents and rhythms.

When the silky, murderous voice finished its rant the television went silent; there was not even the sound of static.

"It…it sounded sort of…well sort of like Greek…" Melissa ventured.

"No, I don't think so," the Professor murmured, combing crumbs out of his beard with his stubby fingers. "If we succeeded in recording it, we shall make its translation one of our plans of campaign." He looked around. "So this is my daughter's room."

"You've been in here many times, Dad," she said. "Bursting in on me to tell me something that could easily have waited."

"Been in here but never really looked," he said. "Not really."

The room contained raw wooden shelves of books on two sides; stacks of books functioned as bookends upholding more shelves. In one corner, a zig-zaggy tower of old magazines: the entire print run of *Visions*. The third wall was dominated by an elaborate home-made shrine to the Shekinah, the feminine spirit of wisdom: a dozen goddess figures, Hindu and Greek and others, surrounded a Black Madonna; a black skinned, Africanized Mother Mary. The corners of the room hung with dusty violet and green scarves, and the table next to the bed was scarred by fallen sticks of incense. Opposite the shrine was a poster of a movie star, Jason Stoll, whom I hated the instant I saw him on Melissa's wall. He was young, muscular, sensitive-eyed, confident, dressed in fashionable understatement. Every girl needs one, I thought.

The books, crammed in every which way, mostly novels and old textbooks—she'd had three years of liberal arts—and obscure volumes of "forgotten lore" her father had given her.

Someone screamed, long and bubbling, from the hall-way. There was a desperate pounding on the front door... which stopped abruptly.

Our feelings had been frozen, looming over us like a stop-motion tsunami, until that instant. Now the film ran forward and all those feelings crashed down on the three of us. People may well react differently to the same stimulus. But we all felt the same thing and knew we felt it together; as if steel chains had been kept in some freezer somewhere, and then clapped onto us all at once; and we all shrank, at the same moment, from the icy shackles.

Melissa spoke in the coiled silence. "Dad…" Her voice was small. "Is it some sort of Armageddon?"

He hesitated only a moment. "I do not believe it is."

I looked at him in surprise. He nodded. "Yes, I mean that. I do not believe it is Armageddon, Biblical or otherwise."

"But," I asked, "what do we do, then? I mean—if we don't just wait for…"

Paymenz reached into a stack of books and pulled out *The New Oxford Annotated Bible*, and flipped expertly to the passage he wanted. He read it aloud.

"Book of Job, chapter five, verse 17: 'How happy is he whom God reproves; therefore do not despise the discipline of the Almighty. For he wounds but he binds up; he strikes but his hands heal.'" He put the book on the bed. Laid his hand thoughtfully on it. "We go with the assumption that all this is happening for a reason. Whatever happens—there is an appropriate response. A lawful response. Along with the natural reactions—fear, anger, whatever you feel. Even during the holocaust there was an appropriate response, when physically fighting back was not possible. Even then, seeing your children taken away and murdered, there was a spiritually appropriate response. Hard to enter into the state where that response is possible, sometimes. But it can be done. We will find the appropriate response."

"And just now?" I asked.

"Now? Now—the appropriate response is to search for the appropriate response. That means research. Scholarship is our sword."

I didn't believe a word of it, but it was good to hear him say it.

"But there's a more pressing concern," Melissa said.

"Yes?" her father said, looking at her.

"Should we try to help those who are being murdered out there?"

We all three turned and stared at the door.

*   *

We went to the kitchen; I climbed up on the edge of the sink and peered out a lower corner of the kitchen window, expecting a feathery spiderleg to ram in through the glass the moment I lifted my head into sight; picturing it plunging a hook into my eye, digging for my brain. But the creatures on the balcony were quiescent, immobile, maybe dormant.

The city, below, was reeling from the invasion. It made me think of footage I'd seen of the bombing of Seoul in 2007: dim, smoke-shrouded canyons of streets lit only by random bonfires and burning cars, and now and then a burning storefront.

Below, now, figures darted for cover. A car careened, something clinging to the roof, flailing at it; the car piling into a hydrant, water geysering, the door torn aside, a man scooped out like a sausage from a can.

Above... Was that a passenger jet, just under the lowering cloud cover? Was it veering in the sky? Was there something that ravaged aboard it?

I climbed down, my mouth gone paper dry again. Melissa looked the question at me. She was hugging herself to keep from wringing her hands.

"It's not good," I said. Meaning, it was still going on, out there—so it was going on in the building; in the hall.

She nodded, biting her lip.

The professor and I armed ourselves with a baseball bat, and a long piece of old pipe left by some plumber behind the water heater. We went to the door to the corridor, and bent

41

near it to listen. There was a thrashing noise and then a steady thumping, sounded to me like it was from the apartment across the hall. Someone shouting for Allah. *Pleading* for Allah. Then—just the thumping, the sound having developed a *wet* quality.

The professor said, "No. Come." He turned on his heel and, breathing hard, went back to Melissa's bedroom and switched on the TV. He changed channels until he found another report. We followed him in.

"We need to know..." he began. But someone on TV finished the remark for him:

"...Can they be killed? We are about to find out..."

You know from the reality programming shows how real-life action looks on television. It hasn't got the good camera angles, or the impressive splashing of the squibs, or the special effects explosions, or even great visual crispness —the image is washed out, badly lit. It looks herky-jerky and uncertain. Half the time a cop tackling a criminal looks like a guy playing football with one of his friends. It's a lot of off-balance fumbling and it's over so quick you can't make out what happened.

But there were at least a dozen in the SWAT team. The demons—five Sharkadians, that I could count, and a Grindum—were all over one of those small school buses they use for mentally handicapped kids, and the kids were in there, slow kids and Down Syndrome kids and deeply pathological kids, a yellow box of them on wheels. The SWAT advanced toward them firing, with some confidence —advancing with something like gleeful *esprit* perhaps because the demons had no guns and because they were feeling the impact of the rounds—knocking them back, skidding them off the bus. The commentator, sounding a bit drunk, saying something about a game a lot of us had played in childhood, *Doom*, and how *Doom* might've been designed like some kind of pre-monition to prepare us for this—

And then a Grindum that had been knocked down by a swarm of bullets simply stood up, and advanced against a stream of gunfire, jerked a gun from a wilting cop's hand, melting the gun in its own claw, and, as the man turned, took him by the throat and forced the molten metal of his gun—bullets exploding—down his throat. The others were running—or were being pulled apart, like flies in the hands of sadistic children—I could see no wounds on the demons though bullets hailed into them.

The Grindum bounded on its giant-grasshopper's legs back to the bus, lunged inside and began to snap confused little heads off in its jaws...

We switched the television off and put our pipe and our baseball bat aside.

No. They cannot be killed. They can be inconvenienced with weapons; they can be slowed down, and forced to reconstitute themselves, if you shatter them sufficiently, but they cannot be killed by any conventional means: more proof that they are supernatural creatures, if any were needed.

* *

One night, in 1986. I'm ten years old, and something has awakened me, and I can't get back to sleep. I thrash in the bed. It's June, and neither warm nor cold, but the sheets seem to abrade my skin and the air seems heavy over my bed, I can feel it pressing on my eyelids. The noise from the living room woke me, I suppose. But it's not the noise that's keeping me awake, it's a kind of shiver that pulses through the house from down there. It's my mother. I can feel her down there, shaking with anguish, although—I know this from past experience—she's probably curled up in a chair staring at the TV, not visibly shaking at all. Now and then she'll uncoil, with a whiplash movement, like an eel on a hook; I've seen it, many times, already this year. But once more I get out of bed and, wearing only my briefs, I go to the second floor landing in our half of the divided Victorian, and look down the worn wooden stairs at Mom in the living room.

It's the amphetamines, I know, confirming it to myself as I see her sit very still, then thrash herself to another position in the chair; then sit very still again. She's staring at the television. She's flicking it with the remote. Channel. Another, another. Channel for five, ten seconds. Another.

Suddenly she stiffens and jerks her head around—I pull back but she's seen me. "Git on down here," she says. She grew up in a trailer park in Fresno; though she's a relatively educated woman she slides back into trailer park diction easily. "Come on come on come on, git down here."

I go down, trailing my hand on the banister. "I woke up. I couldn't get back to…"

"You think I'm weird, don't ya baby?" she said, as I come to the bottom of the stairs. I sit down there and hoped she'd let me stay there. She didn't usually get violent, but she scares me when she's stoned. I wonder where Boyfriend Thing is.

The high ceilinged room is lit only by the TV; the shifting images made the shadows of the room jump like dancing grey-white flames. *Picture-flames*, I think to myself.

I notice that except for the Van Gogh posters—my Mom had a Van Gogh fetish—the room is more barren than it was. Something's missing. The easy chair is there, the vinyl at the end of its arms partly peeled away; the TV, and a thin-metal TV tray with its handful of rattling pot seeds, all that is left of Boyfriend Thing's pot stash—there's no other furniture: The sofa is missing. A nice brown leather sofa. She'd begun to sell things off about then.

"You didn't answer me. You think I'm weird. You do."

"No."

"You do. Because of…because I stay in the house so much now, you told your sister that. When she called." My sister had moved out; she was fourteen and she lived with my aunt. Sometimes I wanted to go. "Well. Well well well. The world is an evil place, Ira. The world is sick and dangerous. You know what they just had on the news? I just saw it. Little girl chained to her bed for five years. She was six years old. That's what kind of world it is."

The irony isn't lost on me at the time. My Mom a speedfreak flipping about someone else's child abuse. But I know now, it was Jung's shadow; the shadow projection.

"In Southeast Asia, this one country, people are, like, just, chopping each other, just hundreds and hundreds, and hiding the bodies…Oh and in Cambodia not that long ago, okay…" She tells me in too much detail about the Killing Fields. "You know what it is?" she says, coming to the question without a pause. "There's demons loose on the Earth pretending to be people. And I'll tell you what—I saw this thing just now, the astronauts can see. They can see from orbit, whenever they're over the night side of the Earth, they can see lightning somewhere every few seconds. Always lightning bashing around somewhere on the Earth, every few seconds. You know what that is?"

I nod, but she's already gone on. I had gotten very skilled, the past few months, at not seeing her face when she was stoned. It was so *puppetlike.* Her eyes, when she was stoned, looked like those glass disks, like flattened marbles, they use for stuffed animal eyes; her skin looked taut as polished wood; her mouth seemed to clack like a puppet's.

"Those flashes they see from orbit, it's lightning is what it is, is all," she is saying, "I'm not crazy, I don't think it's anything else. But I'll tell you what it's *like*. It's like the astronauts are seeing the flash of someone doing something cruel, some big cruelty. An atrocity, like; there *should* be, if there was any fucking justice, some kinda ol' flash or something you could see from space. Maybe it is, maybe there's one lightning flash for every atrocity, somewhere on the Earth. Ought to be. You think I'm weird? You do. Go back to bed. Go on. I've gotta…go on, go on, get your ass up there, go, go…"

I was thinking of that night, listening to my mother's speed rambling, when the Professor turned the televangelist on. The tube preacher was gassing on and on. He was using all his skills. His face was puppetlike; his eyes like glassy disks. And he was babbling but he didn't have his usual confidence. This was Reverend Spencer, I'd seen him before, and he usually strutted with confidence.

Tonight Reverend Spencer looked scared.

"It's occurred to him," the professor said.

"What?" I asked. I sat on the end of the bed sipping tokay wine. It had grown quiet outside…Some sort of lull…

"All the crust he's built up, to hide what he knows in his heart, has been clawed away by what's happening around the world," the professor said.

"I'm hungry," Melissa said, her voice muffled under the pillow she was holding over her head. She was lying in an S shape on the bed behind us. "But if I eat I'll throw up."

Without looking at her, Paymenz reached out and patted her shoulder.

I said, speaking slowly: "You mean, Israel...that it occurred to him...that if this is Judgment Day then he's going to be among the first cast into his favorite lake of fire..."

A news flash had said there was a flurry of televangelists giving away their money.

The professor nodded. He was half listening to the televangelist but his mind was mostly somewhere else.

The professor shut off the television, stood up abruptly, and went into his bedroom-office next door. I could hear him pull a book off the shelf, and turning pages.

We slept only fitfully that long, static night.

I had a dream of a laughing man in a hooded cloak with a face like shifting, running sand—beach-sand that sometimes shifted into the well-sculpted shape of a fairly ordinary human face and sometimes crumbled to reform into the face of a chimpanzee.

He was laughing, but laughing sadly, his voice echoing in the high school gymnasium where we sat in the bleachers, he and I; my echoes mingled with his when I suddenly spoke up: "You're laughing but really you're quite sad, like one of those songs about being a clown when you really want to cry."

"Yes," he said, sobering suddenly. "I am the one who brings sleep and dreams. And what has happened to the world? Who has vomited their colors all over my canvas? Where my art now? Where my art now, I ask you?"

His tears eroded his head so that it sagged off his neck and crumbled into a stream of sand that slithered down over the wooden bleachers.

4

Not long before dawn, as Melissa sank into a doze, I found a sketchbook and pastels I'd given her; she'd never used it, so I did. It kept my mind occupied in the taut, weary hours of the night. I tried drawing everything but the demons, but could find no rest in avoidance. So I tried drawing what would later be called a Sharkadian, and found myself sketching a sort of bas relief pattern, or something like Morris wallpaper, around it, locking it in...

"That's not a bad thing to experiment with," the professor said, his words slurring a little. He'd been at the vodka. "You're unconsciously, if it is unconscious, fitting them into some kind of pattern; making some kind of artistic sense of them since no other offers. And who knows what such a process might divulge..."

But I soon put the sketchbook aside, exhausted and irritated by his occasional critiques; and perhaps troubled by the fear that he was clutching at straws in suggesting the drawing was something useful. Nothing seemed useful, anymore, except a deep hole to hide in.

About nine a.m. the next morning was the first of the Lulls. During Lulls the demons seemed to vanish, or to go into some kind of dormancy, in dark places. They were not sleeping—those who could be seen seemed to be listening.

It was a global Lull. The riots and panicky surges of refugees—who ran into as many demons as they escaped—stopped in their tracks, when the demonic attacks ceased, for a time; the refugees wondering which way to jump. Wondering if angels were next, Michael wielding a fiery sword. The world sank onto its haunches and let its shoulders sag as it panted for breath and wiped its brow.

During the first Lull there was time for pundits to argue on television. Back then they were still babbling the tediously familiar polemic of denial, with their "not demons but anarchists in rubber suits, bullet proof vests, cyborg enhancement"; with their "hallucinations, and the hallucinating attacking people, some of them in costume and makeup ...water poisoned by terrorists..." With their "mind control projections combined with bombings".

Then there was the inevitable counter suggestion: The demons are indicators that the moment has come for complete resignation and submission to God (or Allah or angry ancestral spirits or Yahweh or...Lord Satan). Long lines formed outside churches, synagogues, Buddhist temples; and outside both the Church of Satan, and the First Church of Interstellar Contact—this latter an extraterrestrial contactee outfit run by channelers. It was a riot of metaphysical confusion.

Only Paymenz and a few others kept their heads.

"We will go to the Council For Global Interdependence," said Paymenz, to me. "We need an objective. That will be our first one."

"What," I asked, eating bread and jam in the bedroom. "is the Council for...whatever?" Most of my attention was bent to sounds from the drainpipes on the outer walls that might have been the clicking of large claws.

"CFGI. The Council For Global Interdependence. It's not much of anything yet—it's just a gleam in Mendel's eye.

But there are real contacts there and I was preparing to go over there yesterday morning—it happens that the very day of the Demonic Coming about seventy representatives from twenty countries came to town for a conference funded by the Council. Shephard's conference, actually. One that's not going to go on, but...Most of the conferees are here and may be in the convention center yet...And Shephard..." His voice trailed off. He looked at me but said nothing; I was thinking the same thing:

Hadn't Shephard suggested perhaps that the conference wouldn't happen?

Paymenz seemed to shake himself and went on, "The Council is sheer talk so far—but it represents those who've made other initiatives..."

He sipped his tea. I saw his eyes wander to a vodka bottle leaning precariously on one of Melissa's stacks of magazines; but he looked resolutely away from it. Melissa was sleeping—twitching in her sleep. She would sleep for five minutes, til something unspeakable would drive her out of the dream, and she would sit up... and then sink slowly back.

"What sort of initiatives?" I asked.

"Hm?"

"You said 'those who made other initiatives'?"

"The initiatives...well, it actually began in the middle of the last century. Or perhaps much earlier...But most notably, the formation of the League of Nations, and then the United Nations. Then came the U.N. Peacekeeping force—the NATO actions in Kosovo, the global peace-keeping forces in East Timor. A slow movement toward a real global society with real global policemen; with uniform human rights rules...And it was not all as spontaneous as it seemed. It was planned, as much as it could be. They didn't know that the Indonesians would do what they did in Timor—but they knew what to do if a situation like that arose. And they did. The Council is another project of those same planners. I was one of many consultants. It's something still in its infancy; still unformed and tentative. It could go very wrong—or it could be something wonderful. At any rate, my boy, that's what I'd have said a few days ago. Now, all considerations of the future are subject to redefinition. The future itself is problematic. All of our paradigms are in ruins. Let us go, however...Wake my poor daughter, and let us go to the Council..."

* *

Late afternoon. The sky was lowering with smoke and haze; it looked as if the world was roofed in shale. We were in my converted Chevy Prism—it had been converted to an electric car about ten years before, and never seem to've reconciled to the change. The body was a little too heavy for the electric engine, and it strained to reach 40. I was driving, the Professor beside me; Melissa in the back, leaning forward between the seats.

A burning garbage truck careened around the corner—I pictured it as a Leviathan leaping from the surface of a sea of trash, a burning metal and rubber whale thrashing in and out of the oceanic swells of debris and decay at one of those really enormous landfills. It curveted on two wheels into the middle of our street, streaming flaming trash, its driver a black man with a bottle in one hand, laughing and weeping—I had to drive onto the broad sidewalk to avoid it. The truck was soon out of sight behind us.

"We've got the wrong car for this," I said, as we swerved around another drunken cadre of looters banging and bumping a shopping cart full of holo-set players. "You need one of those hydrogen-powered SUVs—Oh shit..."

This last as an Arab with a rage-contorted face slammed a teenage boy onto the hood of our car—he'd backed him out of his half demolished liquor store, was digging his rigid fingers into the boy's neck. I had to hit the brakes to keep from dragging them down the street—Melissa yelling out the window, "Stop that, stop that, let him go!" The frustrated Arab, seeing his shop destroyed by looters, finally had one in his hands and his face was—oh yes—demonic as he slammed the boy's head on the hood of my car. He was enraged—but was he possessed? No.

No, no one was possessed. Not exactly. There have been no possessions...

Have I said that before? I say it again. It means something.

The boy flailing and the Arab smashing, the two rolled off the car's hood.

"Help them!" Melissa yelled.

I looked at Paymenz. "No," he said, "Drive on. We must get there..."

Driving on, past a group of children throwing bricks through the window of a storefront, I remembered the game —HACKK. A first-person computer game I'd been addicted to...

In HACKK, a biowarfare virus that attacked the human brain turned most of the population into murderous zombies. They were controlled by Terrorist Overlords. You had to get through the smoking ruins of the city, to a sanctuary on the far side, killing psychotic ax-wielding viral zombies as you went, with weapons you picked up along the way, while outsmarting the Terrorist Overlords. It had been superbly realistic 3-D, in which every adversary was a distinct, cunning individual, and yet it had been dreamlike, had the tantalizing familiarity of some half remembered nightmare.

"Who was it," I wondered aloud, as we veered down a mostly empty street—smoking ruins on one side, shattered plastic boxes trailing from store windows on the other—"who said that some video games had the quality of the bardos? E.J. Gold, I think…"

"You're doing that nervous irrelevant commentary again," Melissa said, her voice tight with fear as we drove through gathering shadows.

"Let him say whatever gets him through, here," Paymenz said.

I was driving as I was speaking, as if in a trance. I was so tired. "Remember Gold? One of the last century's grass-roots, homegrown California gurus. He used the game *Quake* to induce a kind of paranoia-sharpened awareness in his followers, told them to think of the bardo states that would come after death as computer games set up by some mysterious programmer. Or *something* along those lines. Learn the rules of that bardo and you'd find your way out, pass the test into the next realm…the next level…"

What were the rules for *this* game? Were we in an afterlife bardo, here?

It wasn't that, either. Demons or no, this was life in all its homely grit, its panoramas of blandness and grainy contrast. Still, there were rules to define, in the new world erupting around us, rules as if from some mysterious programmer. And that had always been true—but now that truth was prominent, unhidden, demanding notice. *You're taking part in a game the rules of which you do not understand! Find out the rules! Now!*

We passed through streets, then, that seemed untouched, distinguished only by the lack of human activity. No moving cars, everyone still hiding.

But two blocks from the convention center, we saw something big and black and steaming from vents on its knobby head, crouched just within the shattered-glass cube of a gas station. Just caught a glimpse of it, dormant in the lull, and then we were past it—driving those last two blocks at the best speed the whiny little car could muster—and reached the convention center, near the Yerba Buena Gardens. A chopper was landing on its helipad as we approached. I watched raptly as it came in, its movements professionally smooth, landing easily—the helicopter was civilization embodied for me, in that moment: civilization intact, confident, almost graceful. It was so reassuring.

"That might be Mendel," Paymenz said, watching the chopper.

"Watch out, dammit, Ira!" Melissa yelled, and I slammed on the brakes, swerved, just managed not to rear-end a white limo pulling up at the police barriers ahead of us.

I sat with my foot still jammed down on the brake, panting, staring at the opaque windows of the limo. Gently, the professor reached over and put the car in park for me; he turned the key, switched the engine off.

The building was modern, highly designed—one of those buildings you imagined on its drawing board and table model, when you saw it—but on the whole it was shaped like a giant bunker, with frills: a concoction of beveled concrete and big panes of frosted glass and angular assemblies of painted girders. There were fidgeting cops standing behind cement barriers around the building, many of them swaying where they stood, probably drunk; others seeming grateful they had something to do that they could understand: crowd control, though there was no crowd.

A cop approached us, his beefy face blotchy red, his mouth open, breathing hard. "You…you people—just turn around…"

"Officer? It's okay," said a tall—*very* tall—black man getting out of the limo. He wore a gray three-piece suit cut so masterfully that it made this man, who must have been more than seven feet tall, seem to have normal proportions. His movements had a touch of the mantis about them, but his dark, African face was chiseled out of quiet intelligence, and his every word emanated simple authority. The cop evidently knew who he was—he walked away without another word.

"Dr. Nyerza," Paymenz said, to the giant African, getting out of the car.

"Professor Paymenz," said Nyerza, nodding. A soft equatorial accent. "It has been too long, sir."

They shook hands. I thought that Nyerza seemed a little amused, looking Paymenz over; but it was not a condescending amusement, it was affectionate.

"I have gotten old, as you see," Paymenz said, signaling for me and and Melissa to get out of the car. "But you still seem...no, not the student I had, your maturity is evident... but still quite boyish."

"Boyish at seven foot four? I enjoy the concept, sir. This is your daughter, perhaps? I am charmed. And—this young man?"

"He is—his name is Ira. He is here as my assistant."

I was feeling numb. I was happy to be his assistant. He could have said, *"This is my trained monkey, we're going to teach him to ride a tricycle across a high wire today,"* and I wouldn't have blinked. Maybe he *did* say that.

"You all look so very tired," the tall black man said. "The emotions we have all had, it's very draining, is it not? There are refreshments. Leave the car where it is, and I will have someone move it to safety. Come this way, please."

*   *

We were walking down a long hallway. We passed a glass door through which I could see an enormous auditorium where groups of querulous people argued with the man at the podium in flagrant disregard for protocol. I couldn't make out most of what they were saying; I caught only crusts and spatters of sentences. "...the Islamic Front claims...the result of prayers—who are we to say it's not...Let each man seek out his own salvation... perhaps sacrifice...the collective unconscious...quantum creations...We're fools...dead minutes from now, everyone here...Hysteria won't..."

"There's food in the private conference room," Nyerza was saying. "But I must prepare you: first, we will pass by a Gnasher. I have just come from observing another one with a Tailpipe at the university."

"These don't sound like scientific terms to me," Melissa said. Somehow, then, she had an air of speaking just to see if she still could.

And in fact Nyerza seemed surprised she'd spoken. "No—already a slang has arisen for the various demons. Reports indicate six kinds so far. One of the creatures has remarked that there are seven expected. The Seven Clans, he said."

"You call them creatures," Paymenz said. "Is this an evaluation on your part? Apart from 'creatures' as in the created of God, the word has implications of..."

"...Of the confines of the biologically conventional, or perhaps extraterrestrial. So I use it wrongly. It is an incarnate spirit, in my opinion. A malevolent spirit, these."

"Demons."

"Quite. Here—I warn you, when we pass the Gnasher, and the Tailpipe—in this room...The Lull may end, they may attack..."

Outside the room were six young National Guardsmen, three of them black, two Hispanic and one a chinless, spindly

Caucasian; they looked as if they were debating between accepting a probable death, when the Lull was over, or desertion.

It was a large conference room, empty but for video screens filling one wall and an oval conference table. The room was windowless; a skylight threw an increasingly rusty light on everything. The table should have collapsed under the weight of the creature occupying most of its surface—the big demon was a Tailpipe, one of those we'd seen squatting in the gas station, something like a pilot whale out of water, but its body was even blunter, curled cobralike in on itself. Nestled in one of its coils was a Gnasher, using the bigger, duller demon as a sort of beanbag chair.

The Gnasher was the color of a red and black ant; its head exactly that red, almost like colored vinyl, its body exactly that black. Its head sat on its pipe of a neck like an ant's, but it had a man's jaws, although oversized, and gnashing, clashing loudly between sentences, like some exotic metallic percussion instrument—and its eyes were those of a man, the pretty blue eyes of a movie star, and its corded arms were lean and there were four of them and they were leathery black. The Gnasher lifted its head languidly as we looked in and, unexpectedly, began to speak. It spoke at length to us—Nyerza took a step back at this. We stood in the open doorway and listened to the demon as it spoke. Its hands were talons and only talons; impossibly prehensile claws that rippled delicately like a Balinese dancer's fingers to emphasize its words. It had an enormous phallus, armored in big, spurred scales—I couldn't see the rest of its lower parts.

"We should have a tape recorder going—this is the first time it has spoken," Nyerza murmured to Paymenz.

"I'll remember every word," I said, my voice sounding whispery, husky in my own ears.

"Ira has a photographic memory," Paymenz muttered.

The demon, reverberating on: **"...I am so delighted to see you, I feel the delight as a violet fire on the roof of my mouth as I look at you, and I stiffen with recognition..."** Its voice was a languid purr, but every word stood out like billboard copy printed on the projection screen of the inside of my skull. **"This is the joy of homecoming! How long we waited, forgotten children in a forgotten nursery, weeping for our return to those who left us to ripen in the outer darkness; whose patented-polymer members drove the seed into the soil of the in-between; my dear dears how we hungered for the taste of your light, the one spark that each of you carries, that each of you monstrously denies to us; how you hoard your little sparks, her fallen sparks—hers not yours, little dears, but it's all 'finders keepers' with you!—and for a moment when we return to the source of our course, and we pluck the fruit, and we draw the root, and we consume the harvest, in one sweet bite, or two at most, and we taste the spark, we have the spark, then, within us. Oh, for but a moment. Before it flickers out...before it flickers out, snuffing itself like a sniffing little snob; before it goes, the spark of your inner light warms the infinite cold of our withins: for a moment the aching emptiness is abated, and we can pretend we are the created and not the residue, and the journey is fulfilled; and then the spark flickers and is gone and we must search again for another morsel. And how does the song go?"**

As it paused to consider before reciting something like verse, I thought: *This is stupid, I should be running, hiding, and the only reason I'm not is because Melissa is here, watching me. And she would not run with me; she is so much braver than I am.*

It seemed to savor, for a moment, the sound of one of the National Guardsmen weeping senselessly to himself, before theatrically clearing its throat to go on:

"Consider this:

His eyes are white-light ceiling bulbs,

his teeth syringe-needles

he's attended by a retinue of shiny scarab beetles

I stood a-teetering on the vacuum-breathing brink

where you fall with the weight of a single thought you think... (it's very good, don't you think? But to continue...)

where laughing things rise to find they truly sink

and white on white on white on white is the color of my ink

I didn't pass through the tunnel, the tunnel passed through me

death will not hesitate to come unseasonably ...

It takes joy in coming unreasonably...

"I remember death—I remember death, oh but yes:

I've bargained with that smug old merchant of rest

though that time is past, and I pretend we never met

you know what hasn't happened—will, onward, happen yet...

"I no longer taunt the lion, nor will I walk the edge

I withdrew from the void that shimmers past
the ledge
But every morning when I wake
I see the shadows smile
I know that it is but his whim to bide a while..."

The demon's mouth split his head in something like a
smile. It seemed to me the demon was looking at Melissa,
as he spoke...It seemed to me...as it went on,

"What do you think? One of your minor poets? Almost doggerel, in fact. But I like it. Because the fear of death is the tenderest thought
you have for such as us; your forlorn offspring.
The only elegy we have is your fear, your anticipa-
tion of darkness, and so we savor it, out of sentiment, sheer sentiment. How like the fish you are;
swimming in the sea but unaware of it; you are the
fishy swimmers awash in a sea of suffering!
Waves of suffering break over us—to me, like the
fragrance of a meal as it is cooked—how we mimicked you in our stony world, making meals over
campfires when we could, and appointing chief-
tains, and kings, and holding pageants—if you
could see the pageants of our world, and how you
were celebrated there!"

"What is your mission here?" Paymenz demanded suddenly. "What brought you here? Speak plainly!"

The demon simply ignored him, continuing: "... And
now you at last acknowledge us, haughty till we
squeeze her spark from you, and we are for a
moment more truly one, and—how did it go—'what
do I see, in the dusty mirror? Not a human being
but a human error'...And so we rectify, we return
what you have supposed to be excrescence, to
make you whole again, to rejoin, to warm our-

selves with the singled-out sparks until the great spark, the tongue of flame that will not flicker out, is revealed to us. We shall turn our faces up to it...No longer taking part in your world by proxy but a part of you as you become part of us..." Saying this last its voice began to boom, to make the very walls recoil in shivers, and it stood up . . . **"A part of us, a part of us, the infinite loneliness brought to an end, the serpent with its tail in its mouth swallows, at long last! He swallows and swallows in infinite repercussion!"**

And the Tailpipe began then to uncoil, to rear up, and its slick black skin opened pores which oozed something like petroleum and something like sewage sludge, and I saw then that the pores were something else: they were the mouths of little girls, pink and perfect, complete with teeth and tongues, hidden before and now exposed and expressing black rivulets...and then steam, steam in place of the black ooze, hissing and smelling of sea-trenches and filling the room with a congealing cloud of hot mist.

One of the Guardsmen screamed and fired his weapon twice at the Gnasher. The demon's mouth spread in a caricature of a grin as it turned toward the babbling soldier, and something blurry whipped out from the Tailpipe and encircled the young soldier, who was yanked instantly through the air to the Gnasher, who held him nose to noseless face, the soldier screaming as the Gnasher said, **"Look— it's *magic!* It's *your bullets!* See them!"**

I could just make them out—the two rounds the soldier had fired were floating within the Gnasher's eyes, pointed at him, cartoonishly replacing its pupils. The Gnasher moved—its movements too fast to follow: Then the soldier had no head.

The other soldiers began to fire, and Nyerza was pulling the Professor and I back from the demons, from that mist-choked room; I thought I heard the Gnasher call, *"Melisssssssaaaa!"*

Then we were running down the hall—I looked back to see one of the soldiers, the spindly one with hardly any chin, his mouth all twisted up like a little boy trying not to cry, wanting to run after us but a lifetime of fantasized heroism holding him back, quivering there in the dirty mist that rolled from the door into the hallway, and then he ran into the room and was instantly killed—in a split second, his blood, most of it, flew back out the door and onto the corridor wall, as if tossed from an offstage bucket, and I heard his last cry, a cry for Mama though no word was articulated: the echo of a million million cries of suffering that had been going on for thousands of years, and I felt like an adult who sees a small child caught by spreading fire in a room, and the adult, who is not uncaring, chooses between himself and the child and runs out the front door, knowing that the child will die. I felt I had abandoned a child to a cruel death.

All the Guardsmen were dead, soon after, for the Lull was over, and then the Gnasher and the Tailpipe moved into the auditorium, and managed to kill a good third of them before the survivors fled beyond reach. Beyond reach, for the moment.

* *

We were in a basement conference room. The demons might materialize here; but they didn't. There was a cafeteria buffet on a big military folding table, but none of us could eat, though the professor drank some wine.

Nyerza was wearily saying something about patterns, patterns, patterns noticed already, geographical patterns in the arrival of the demons. "It is not really at random, no not at all. It is around certain urban areas, like the 'rays' from an impact crater on the moon, really, lines of them spreading out from a center, in which is…Do you remember the industrial accidents, last year?"

Nyerza and Paymenz were near the barred door of the dull concrete room; a chilly room, with unpainted gray walls, pipes crisscrossing the ceiling; Nyerza standing, leaning against the wall, as most chairs were unsuitable for him, Paymenz sitting crosslegged on a plastic chair too small for him, hidden by his bulk so that he seemed to be seated on air, with a carafe in one hand and a plastic cup in the other, drinking and talking, one knee bobbing nervously; looking sickly pale under the fluorescent tube lights. There was a chunky black SFPD cop standing guard at the door, staring wistfully at the wine bottles on the table, chewing his lip. Nyerza was lighting an oval cigarette. The cop almost said something to him about it—then I saw him shrug. Demons were tearing up the city—and he was going to give him shit about the no-smoking rule?

Melissa and I were seated on two plastic chairs; I had my arm around her; she leaned against me. It was more need for mutual comfort than anything intimate.

I wanted to tell her something.

If the end is coming, we should be somewhere else, making love, and enjoying one another, and, perhaps, praising God for whatever good there has been in our lives; grateful for one another and the goodness of our last moments together . . .

But I knew I probably wouldn't say it. And if I did it would avail me not.

Suddenly she interrupted Nyerza and Paymenz, who stared at her as she said, "That poem he recited…"

64

"Yes, do you know the author? It might hold a clue..." Paymenz said.

"Yes I do. It's actually a song lyric. I'm the author."

"You!"

"Yes. It's a song I wrote, two years ago, when I was in that folk group, 'The Lost'..." She was staring at her hands on her knees. "I was going through a depression, when I wrote it, and a sort of...I was almost as morbid as Ira. And then—the demon looked at me, and recited it: A song I wrote...Wrote thinking about how my Mom died, and how death doesn't care if it comes at a, you know, reasonable time, and it just took my Mom and I..." She stared wonderingly into space and repeated, "That thing recited a song I wrote..."

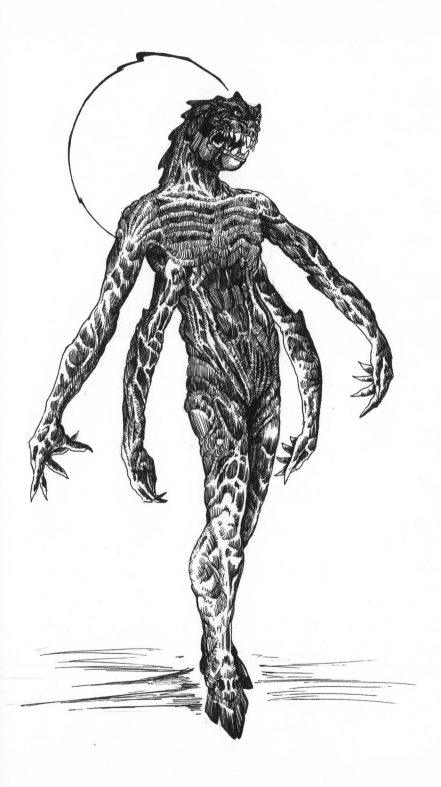

5

They'd brought two folding cafeteria tables down into the basement room, pushed them together and spread taped-together print-outs over their formica tops. "Please forgive this hasty presentation," Nyerza said as he smoothed the print outs with his enormous hands. We were gathered around the tables, the Professor and Melissa and Nyerza and myself.

I was noticing his frequent glances at Melissa. He was suddenly very interested in her. She seemed drawn to stand close beside him. She glanced up at him, her nostrils quivered; her lips parted; she leaned just half an inch closer to him.

Oh yeah. Like I could compete with a giant black intellectual power-broker from Central Africa.

On the print-outs, taped together with scotch tape where the images connected, was a map of the United States. There were six cities designated in black letters. New York City; Portland, Oregon; San Francisco; Chicago; Miami; Detroit. Concentric circles, in light red, were drawn from each city, as if it were the epicenter of some outrippling force: each city the center of a bullseye. The circles overlapped. Yellow dots marked the map, in rough lines from each city—almost exactly like the impact lines extending out from the center of a lunar meteor strike. The meteor hits the moon, there's a crater, and impact lines out from the crater, in every direction. But the actual "bullseyes" seemed slightly off-centered from the city-marks.

"The yellow dots," Paymenz said.

"Yes," said Nyerza. "The demons. Where they appeared. Thickly in the cities, you see, a bit less extended out in lines from the 'strike points' in certain places in the city. We have here..." He drew another long print-out, like a computer-spun scroll, from a briefcase, and unrolled it over the taped up map. "San Francisco. You see the 'epicenter' of the strike points is over here—an industrial area to the Southeast across the bay..."

"Where the accident happened," I blurted. "Hercules!"

"Yes, the little city of Hercules," Nyerza said. "All but wiped out a few years ago in an industrial accident. Very like what happened in Bhopal, in the last century, I understand. Perhaps you lost friends or relatives there?"

"Nobody. But I have friends who lost relatives there." I thought of Jerry Ingram, whose brother had been killed. I remembered how Jerry had put it: "Wiped out like a bug in pesticides...his whole family wiped out like bugs, his wife and kid wiped out like bugs...fucking bugs, man...bugs..." One of my very few real friends, Jerry. A writer. He'd slipped back into drug use, after that; was supposed to be somewhere in LA.. If the demons hadn't killed him; his own or ours.

"You know," I said, staring at the print-out, "it's very like that artwork I did...I never showed anyone but Melissa ...I used a map of Hercules...and the area around it... And..."

Melissa's mouth dropped open. "God yes, you're right! That is weird—it's so...there's something like that drawing..."

"I've got it, I think, in my palmer…we could hook it up with your printer…" I broke off, feeling foolish. "Oh but—I don't know what the relevance is."

Paymenz looked at me. "Relevance? The lines converge, now, and serendipity, and catastrophic coincidence, my boy, are the order of the day." He turned to Nyerza. "Now we see, Nyerza, that intuition is our only guide in the present situation. And perhaps scholarship… Which reminds me." He searched through a number of pockets till he found the little recording we'd made of the televised demon speaking in his own language. "If you could run this through your best translation programs…Try Sumerian analogues…"

In an adjoining room was a row of workstations. The power was still on, then, and they had no problem loading the contents of my palmer into their system. I did a search through my saved art, scanned drawings mostly. A sketchy portrait of the magician AO Spare flickered by; an image of a pregnant angel giving birth to a demon…

"Interesting," Nyerza muttered, at that.

…a painting of the planets in alignment and a planet-sized being of electrical energies leaping from one to the next, a sketch of Melissa sunning herself nude on a rooftop. I scrolled past that one as hastily as possible but Paymenz said, "Remarkable accuracy." And put a hand in front of his mouth to hide a smile we couldn't see anyway, under the beard.

…and then the drawing: a scan of a map of the town of Hercules, including the refineries, and superimposed over it, using streets for part of its diagramming and other parts drawn in, was…

"A pentagram!" Nyerza said wonderingly. "Turned upside down..."

"Yes—'horns' upward," Paymenz muttered. "Indefatigable, the conjunctions...Synchronicities more meaningful than ever...the atmosphere sensitive...very sensitive..."

I spread my hands, trying to remember how the image had come about. "I had this...this sort of vision of the area of the industrial accident as a kind of...like a sacrificial altar with a pentagram drawn on it. You see the blood around the edges. I felt the people who died in that area had been sacrificed to...I don't know."

"To Mammon," Melissa suggested.

"Perhaps not quite literally Mammon as such," Paymenz murmured. "I wish I had that son of a bitch Shephard here."

Nyerza tapped at the keyboard, and soon had my image superimposed over the map of Hercules with its demon-manifestations...

Which lined up perfectly with the pentagram.

We passed the night in the rooms beneath the conference center. Army cots were brought to us, and Melissa and I lay down near one another, falling asleep almost immediately. There was just time for Melissa, lying huddled under a green blanket, turned away from me, to say, "You're in trouble you know, you sneaky brat. That one drawing of me on the roof...You've got that birthmark on my ass—a naked ass you're not supposed to have had the chance to see...You had to've spied on me when I was up there..."

"One time I was looking for you and you were asleep up there...It was purely by accident...I left immediately."

"Immediately...my ass. You got the goddamn scene awfully...detailed...You..."

"I can't help having a photographic memory."

But she was already snoring; I was asleep moments later.

* *

Nyerza and Paymenz conferred with colleagues by internet, and phone, though some of the lines were down and power came and went. The next morning, in the little room with the print-outs, we ate something an unnatural yellow, something dry and glutinous and salty we were told was reconstituted scrambled eggs.

"We have been working, developing a theory," Nyerza said, hunched in a bass clef over his plate.

"Last night?" Melissa said. "You need rest too, don't you, Dr. Nyerza?"

He smiled shyly at her concern. I tried not stare at her; I ground my teeth.

"I had a few hours, thank you," he said. "Anyway, we theorize that this accident was not an accident, that its parameters were quite calculated. Here, in Detroit—another accident, some years back. In Miami, no accident but there were, instead, what are called, I believe, 'cancer corridors' extending out from the industrial site here...Dr. Mendel believes..."

"I believe they are also not accident," said a short, bald, stocky man with an accent that might've been Dutch. He came in pulling off his overcoat, tossing it on a chair, which fell over with the weight of it. He didn't even glance that way. He was carrying a package, something long and narrow wrapped in brown paper: I thought of a sword in a

71

scabbard, and then I thought, *That's silly, it's not a sword.* He put the package on the table.

Nyerza introduced Dr. Mendel. He had an ageless face, that seemed to have some kind of Oriental cast to it; as if he were perhaps a quarter Asian, and partly—what?—Dutch? German? I guessed he was something like fifty, but it was hard to tell. His eyes were fathomless black. He wore a rumpled gray suit, and simple athletic shoes of some kind; he moved with a strange springiness, as he crossed the room and shook our hands. He seemed tired, but fed by some relentless spring of inner energy. There was an indefinable resilience about everything he did. "Yes," he said, looking at the print outs. "I believe that none of this is an accident. Some happened before others—but each was timed. Some were greater pulsations, some lesser; that is, some events required sudden, widespread loss of life in a small area; with others, slow deaths, even suffering, was preferable. It was planned over a forty year span. Maybe even more. Perhaps Bhopal was the beginning, really. For the demons are in other cities too. But we have focused on this country as a sort of experimental subject in the study..."

"Planned by who?" Melissa asked.

"Now, that is the question. I prefer to wait before speculating too openly...More information is needed."

Who was this man? I wondered. And where was he taking us, with all this?

He had an odd smell about him—not unpleasant. Rather exotic. Was it incense?

"If they were not accidents...these industrial...horrors," I said, slowly, "And if...if the demons are the byproduct...Please—tell us what you think. Speculate. Who planned it? How? What sort of ritual...?"

I was beginning to speak faster and faster, with a growing excitement that fed from hope. Real hope—for if what was happening had an explanation, then it might have a solution. An explanation meant that the universe, life itself, was not some manic absurdity where any random god of chaos could inflict his demons on us. There was hope for an underlying meaning after all...

"I mean—if someone planned it, then there are rules, there are..."

Mendel stopped me with a raised hand, as someone entered. I took it that he didn't want it discussed in front of the new visitor. Paymenz laid some print-outs face down atop those taped to the tables, to hide them.

The visitor was Professor Laertes Shephard, looking exactly as I'd last seen him, though there was a quality in his eyes like a candle, just after it's been snuffed. A glow fading to ash. He came to where we stood at the tables; glanced at them, and away.

"Gentlemen," he said. He looked at Melissa, a disheveled gamin, with what seemed to me like masked longing. "Melissa. I'm glad to see you're...well."

"Alive, you mean," she said.

"Just so." He turned like a turret to Mendel and said, "I will not mince words. I have come to ask you to take part in the Appeasement Program."

"And that would be exactly what, Shephard," Paymenz growled, "and proposed by exactly whom?"

"The Committee on Social Economics, would be the who of it," said Shephard, unruffled.

"Who's that?" Melissa asked.

"Why, my dear," Shephard said, not quite looking at her, "it is a committee of economists and business people who have long been concerned about the world."

"It's an influential 'think tank' of people highly placed in multinationals, and conservative theorists. New Right, that sort of thing," Paymenz said impatiently.

Mendel nodded, adding: "I hope this appeasement is not what I think it is…They cannot be appeased."

"We don't know they cannot be appeased," said Shephard, inclining a stiff little bow toward Mendel. "We hypothesize that perhaps they can. That they can be conceded territory, a certain amount of…sustenance, and if it's offered up in a, shall we say, old fashioned spirit of the sacrificial rite, we may hope to connect with whatever it was that pleased such entities in ancient times."

I looked at Melissa. At Paymenz. He nodded wearily. I asked Shephard, "Are you talking about going to the demons with people—offering them to them as…as offerings…sacrifices? Abasing ourselves? Facilitating the murder of human beings?"

"Do you have a better method, young man, for even so much as slowing them down?"

"It's too soon to say—but I think we'd all be better off dead than doing that. We have our souls to think of."

"Hear him," Mendel said, nodding. "He has gone to the quick of the matter. Shephard: it is unthinkable."

"It is already underway." And he turned and walked out.

"I suspect," Mendel said, "we should have killed him, on the spot."

But no one went after Shephard.

*　*

I sat slumped in a plastic chair, and stared up at the dusty metal pipes tangling the ceiling like a freeway interchange, beginning to feel a real hunger to see the sky. Nyerza and Mendel came over, carrying chairs and a bottle of wine, plastic cups, to sit beside me. I sat up, looking from one to the other, feeling, as they looked at me, like a small animal about to be radio-tagged by two zoologists.

"Uh—yes, gentlemen?"

Mendel said, "When you spoke of the origin of that image—the one that collated so interestingly with the appearances of the demons in that area—you said you had a sort of vision of it?"

"Yes...?"

"When you say 'vision', Ira," Nyerza said, "do you mean, exactly, a...How do you describe..."

I thought about it. "No, not like...Ezekiel. I mean, I envisioned it as an artist, that's all. But it was a very strong visual, um, inspiration, so...I almost think of it as a vision. But it's not like I heard a light from heaven saying, 'Why do you persecute me'?"

"Quite," Mendel said, nodding. He looked at Nyerza. "Even so. And the synchronicities."

"We must make the leap," Nyerza said. "What he and the girl bring us cannot be brought by accident. Their higher selves collaborate with the Higher Design."

"I...wish to make a leap, too," I said. They looked at me, both with eyebrows raised. Nyerza's eyebrows a couple of feet higher than Mendel's. "Israel—Professor Paymenz —he spoke of...an organization. I take it you both belong to it. I took it to be a political organization. Progressive organization of some kind but...You both seem to be involved in something, um...esoteric? I mean in the sense of the three circles—exoteric, mesoteric, esoteric." I thought I saw Mendel suppress a smile and I added hastily, "I don't mean that I *know* these things deeply. But I have some sense of them. I helped the professor edit his book, at one point, and I worked at...well it's just a magazine but..."

"No, the magazine *Visions* was sometimes on the right track," Mendel said. "I occasionally contributed to it under a pen name."

"Which name?" I asked in surprise.

He shook his head, smiling. "Some things you know...I will tell you this much more, which will be some things you have guessed, and heard, and maybe a little more, but, if you trust me, this will serve as a confirmation: In ancient times, well before the birth of Jesus of Nazareth, certain people struggled to became *conscious*—conscious, and not identified with what the Buddhists call samsara, with the false self, the shadows on the wall of the cave...And a few became truly conscious, more or less at the same time. Some were in what we now call Egypt, some in India, some in China, some in what is now Nepal, some in Africa, one in North America—a few others. You've studied enough to know—there are degrees of consciousness, of being awake and mindful, of being aware of oneself and the subtler aspects of one's surroundings and of being aware of the Cosmos itself. You have felt a little of this awareness yourself—almost anyone has had the feeling of being much more awake at some times than at others. Things being more vivid, life lived more in the moment, some greater sense of connectedness. It passes quickly for most people, and they forget it. But there are those who know it can be cultivated and sustained and refined and taken to a very high level—when a certain degree of competence is achieved in this practice, one passes a threshold and becomes truly conscious—as much as one can be as a mortal person, embodied—and when that happens one becomes *psychically* aware of other truly conscious people, though they may be thousands of miles away. Aware of one another, they came together and formed a...what people call a 'secret society' or 'Secret Lodge'. One name for it is the Conscious Circle of Humanity."

"Mendel," Nyerza interrupted. "Are you sure? This boy has earned no such initiation."

"True, but it is only words, dear colleague, and in these extreme circumstances, perhaps everyone with a fertile soul must be initiated to the degree they can be. We need all the help we can get. And there are indications, do not forget, about these two young people...And he is a friend to the Urn..."

"Yes, true, true, go on then, please."

"So," Mendel went on, "The Conscious Circle continued in various forms. Sometimes its members were murdered and decimated by enemies, diabolic forces in various guises. But we continued as best we could. And we evolved a...a sort of plan, an overall scheme. We formed sub-lodges, lesser lodges, which not every member of the sub-lodge understood. For example, we created the original Masonic lodge and the Knights Templar and the original Rosicrucians, and certain circles in the East...But few of the members of those lodges—*even their highest initiates*—were aware of the Conscious Circle, or the real reason for the formation of those lodges. The *real* secret lodge was a circle which kept the other better known lodges as satellites, of a sort. And these lodges were used to promote...for example...the Magna Carta...the Renaissance, and the Enlightenment, and the development of the idea of the Republic. The work of Lao Tzu. The Buddha was one of ours. Jesus of Nazareth—one of our greatest initiates: As much the son of God as any embodied man could be. But his teaching was of course co-opted, and muddied... Thomas Jefferson was one of us. A few others you would know. But most kept to the shadows...There have been experiments, failed experiments. For example, we introduced LSD...And LSD was not supposed to become a street drug and what it led to—ah, we have our failures, you see. We yet hope to guide humanity to a global unity, a democratic unity, a United States of the Earth…"

"But not a unity controlled by the USA," Nyerza hastened to add. "Controlled by representatives of all the nations. Yet far more powerful than the United Nations."

Mendel nodded, and continued, "In our awkward way, and with many false starts, we slowly guide humanity to, we hope, an attitude of tolerance, of social justice, of respect for human rights; and, yes, to the end of war. Ultimately, to a condition which makes for a greater probability of Becoming-Conscious on the part of more people… And, therefore, a condition of service to the Higher, which men often call God… Now, have a glass of this regrettable chablis, and chew that over. You have answered our question, and we have some work to do. God bless you, young man. Pray for us all."

* *

As I write this now, it occurs to me that had anyone else told me the things that Mendel told me, any other time, the skeptic in me—the skeptic shielding the man who deeply yearns to believe—would have nodded politely but inwardly doubted every word. Despite my association with *Visions* Magazine, and my inner certainty that *some* kind of spiritual world is real, I have always been skeptical of most of what people claimed to be the manifestations of that world in our own. The Conscious Circle of Humanity? Another supposedly ancient supposedly secret supposed society? With anyone else, I'd have thought the man was trying to set me up for induction into a cult, or that he'd become delusional and sucked others, like Nyerza, into his delusions, as can happen with the charismatically mad.

But there was a recognition in me, when he told me of the Conscious Circle—and implied his own part in it. There was a certitude in the very air, an understanding in me, a resonance with what he'd said, that somehow transcended all doubts—though others had made similar, rather convincing claims, in my presence, about their own esoteric connections, and those others I had not believed. Here was the real thing, and it was the force of his Being, the very consciousness that he described, that confirmed it to me. I felt it in the air as a man feels a powerful electric field around a hydroelectric generator. I felt it only when he chose to show it to me. But it was quite real.

Later, I drew Paymenz aside. "You know what Mendel told me—about the Conscious Circle?"

"I heard."

"Do they…take students?"

"You would not have been told were you not a serious candidate."

"And…and you, Dr. Paymenz?"

He heaved a great sigh. "Once, Nyerza was my student. Now, I am his student. I was truly conscious, or nearly, for a time. But I…I *fell*. I re-experienced the Fall of Man. I—do not wish to discuss how it came about. My own frailty. Complete consciousness is a burden as well as a kind of enthronement. I now…struggle to return to the kind of consciousness they have. Nyerza and Mendel. And I warn you—to waken, to really waken, is as painful as a birth. And some die in childbirth."

He would say nothing more.

That night, I woke from a nightmare of a Sharkadian raging through an Elementary school, to find Melissa gone from her cot. I got up, went down a hallway where every other light was lit, and even these flickered fitfully. I heard a cry from a room to the side, and thought a demon had dragged her away, to torture her to death there. I looked in, opening my mouth to shout, and saw Nyerza rearing naked over her on his cot, and it was he who cried out, and her face, turned to him, was like the Madonna, and I hastened away, feeling shattered—but hoping they hadn't seen me. No one should transgress on rapture.

6

I'd have laid odds that Mendel, who had, at Nyerza's side, been involved in saving tens of thousands of African refugees from tribal-genocide a few years before...

Who had seemed unafraid, centered in the face of a relentless and immeasurable invasion of apparently inde-structible supernatural predators...

That this man could not be shaken, could not be cowed. But he seemed pale, unnerved, the next morning, as he brought us a report from the translator programs and the industrial-accident investigation.

Before he came...Waiting for Mendel, we sat around the cafeteria tables, drinking acrid coffee...

I was heartily sick of this place but afraid to go any-where else, for we had news from the outside world, some-times: The demons seemed to move in 'fronts' across the land, and whoever escaped and remained behind the wave was safe for a time, until another demonic sweep through that area. People had begun to adapt already, adopting strategies for going on with some semblance of their lives around the demons, behind them, and during the lulls, taking comfort in government announcements of research, of ex-perimental relocations of population to less infested ar-eas—which soon became diabolically infested.

Confrontations and sometimes gun-battles came about between streams of refugees and people housed in those areas used, willy nilly, as refuge—until refugee camps were established.

There were accusations in the fragmentary media, where the cables and fiber optic lines still remained, that attempts had been made, on the part of experimental governmental teams, to sacrifice to the demons, as Shephard had suggested, offering up lifers from prison, volunteers, people whose status was murkily defined; even, according to some stories, homeless children. The demons, it was rumored, took the sacrifices and gave nothing in return. There were official denials that any of this had taken place. Meantime, the slaughter continued; cults formed and were dissolved; militias formed and were dissolved; National Guardsmen roamed in both fanatical order and anarchic melees.

In our underground lair, I sipped my vile coffee; I looked at Nyerza sidelong, now and then, and Melissa, and though they weren't holding hands, I thought, with a stabbing pang: *They are lovers. She is his.*

And told myself : *He's a great man, he deserves her, I don't.*

It didn't help.

That's when Mendel came in carrying a sheaf of print outs. He laid them with trembling hands in front of Paymenz, who seemed surprised, himself, at Mendel's state.

"Are you quite all right, Monsignor Mendel?" Paymenz asked. This was the first and only time I heard him called Monsignor, and it was news to me.

"I…have seen something…a bit of personal precognition…how things will end with me, at least, with my embodiment, and it is…It is not something I wish to discuss. But we have much else to discuss: The demonic declamation, which you recorded from the television, appears to be in a language related both to proto-Sumerian and the most ancient language associated with Egypt..." He turned to his notes and went on, "It translates, to the extent it is translatable, as follows: *Now at last is the long delayed feast commenced; the sheep have been driven to the* [possible translation:] *temple, and the slaughter is* [unintelligible]. *How richly run the* [possible translation:] *gutters, of jade and adamantine. The circle closes; the circle for which this world was created...*[untranslatable] *cleave to my* [untranslatable]...*Our fast is at an end...What astounding pretensions are theirs; how the* [unintelligible] *roll their eyes, how they* [possible translation:] *bleat and try to rise on hind legs like men...How few the men* [or: *"true humanity"*], *and how* [possible translation:] *transient... Come now attendants and brethren and* [untranslatable]..."

Mendel laid the text aside, took a long, slow breath, and looked at the others. "This business about the circle closing, the apparently fore-ordained, fore-planning of it..."

Nyerza shivered visibly. "Perhaps it is...demonic hubris."

"It could be that they knew someone would translate and they sought to demoralize us," Paymenz said.

"It could be," Mendel said. "But deep in my soul there is a dread as never before..."

"What was that line from Dickens," Melissa said. "Something about, are these the shadows of what will be, or may be, if the way to the future is unaltered..."

Mendel smiled fondly at her. "Do you know, I believe that something speaks through you, my dear, something precious."

She looked at him in open mouthed surprise. Then managed, "Sure—Dickens."

Mendel chuckled.

Paymenz shook his head at Mendel. "Do not speak of it yet. Now—as to the industrial accidents…?"

Mendel nodded. "It seems that recently, two to three thousand men and women associated with manufacturing, especially in the chemicals and petroleum fields, have just… disappeared. Indeed: they vanished the night before the demonic attack. And, my friends, each one of them was an executive or key person associated with a company which either had a major industrial accident or was responsible for a long-lasting 'cancer corridor', a record of much death and sickness around their factories, invariably covered up or, I think the expression is, glossed over, by…spinning doctors?"

"Spin doctors," I muttered. "The Conscious Circle— are there those who are…conscious or…or powerful, esoterically powerful…who—who are opposed to…to the Conscious Circle?"

"Yes. It is possible to be conscious but to be sick—to be conscious does not mean to be good," Mendel said. "There are very few such people—only a handful. But there are only 23 Conscious people in the Circle—only 23 *good* conscious people in the whole world, except for a few black magicians."

"Only 23!"

"Your mouth is hanging open, Ira," Paymenz said. "It is a grotesque effect."

"But—how can you know there's only 23?"

"We know," Mendel said dismissively. "As for the sick ones, the dark magicians, they may manipulate hundreds of others, using certain abilities that come to such people when they become conscious. Telepathy, psychic control, and so forth. They have their own agenda, you see—but it is not that they are *opposed* to us particularly. They are indifferent to us so long as we do not get in their way. They wish to make themselves gods. They believe that each can rule his own universe, his own Cosmos—and exploit it for his pleasure, if they become powerful enough."

Paymenz said sadly: "Some people become the apotheosis of selfishness, and call it exalted."

Mendel nodded. "Now as to…" He broke off, looked at the ceiling and frowned. He shivered and buttoned the top buttons of his shirt, though it was quite warm.

Melissa said, suddenly, "I'm worried about my cats, Dad."

Kind of a non sequitur, I thought, but typical of Melissa. The remark was something that I loved her for, though I don't know why.

Nyerza looked at her with lifted eyebrows. "Cats?"

She scowled at him, knowing what he was thinking. "Yes. Cats. I know—the world is being eaten alive. All those people. And I'm worried about my cats. That's just how I am. I need to know they're okay."

"They have water and dry food, my dear," Paymenz said, patting her hand.

Brows knit, Mendel glanced again at the ceiling—then in the direction of the conference room where we'd met the demons.

Nyerza snorted softly, was saying, "Well this is so much American…to be concerned about cats at such a time…"

I looked at Nyerza and thought, with a little flush of mean-spirited triumph: *Being 'awakened' apparently doesn't necessarily make you always compassionate, always empathetic. It doesn't make you perfect. And it doesn't take away lust.*

Nyerza looked at me—I had the uncanny sense that he'd read my mind. I looked away.

"You're quite right," Mendel said, smiling gently at me. Mendel! Not Nyerza. "We are imperfect, even...even then."

Melissa looked at Mendel, then at me. "Ira didn't say anything...Did he?"

Suddenly Mendel lifted his head, and seemed to sniff the air. He looked at Nyerza, and both looked at the ceiling. Then at the hallway.

"The forbearance is at an end," Mendel said.

"Is it?" Paymenz said, going pale beneath his beard. "It was always surprising..."

"What are you *talking* about?" Melissa asked, her voice rising, breaking, the knuckles white on her clenched hands.

I reached out instinctively and took her hand; she let me do it. Her hand opened in mine like a blossom.

She looked at Nyerza, then at me. "Could we...go somewhere and...and talk—Ira?"

Then the screams from above began. The room shook; a subterranean thunder rattled the pipes; plaster sprinkled, then rained down like flour from a sifter.

Nyerza ran to the police guards, shouting.

Drawing their weapons, the men hurried into the hallway, a ramp slanting gradually up to stairs leading to the next floor.

Mendel had slipped away, off to the room he slept in—to hide?

Then a reptilian stench rolled into the room, a wind laden with a palpable reek that seemed to coat the inside of my nose and mouth with viscosity—like the putrid discharge you get on your fingers handling a garter snake.

Nyerza was trying to herd us back, away from the hallway entrance when something rolled down that hallway toward us, down the ramp to our feet, a furry ball: the severed head of one of the guards; then another came rolling down, seconds later, to bump with a wood-block clunk into the first. Someone screamed—I think it was me, not Melissa —and the demons we'd encountered in the conference room upstairs were there: the Gnasher and behind him the great sinuous bulk of the Tailpipe...

I remember thinking: *Just as things are beginning to make sense, chaos comes for me.*

I pulled Melissa back—she sagged on rubbery knees, making it hard to move her—and I wanted Mendel to be there, to explain, to make things rational again—

As if I'd summoned him, Mendel entered the room. At first he seemed the emblem of absurdity: he'd changed into a costume. Mendel carried a silvery broadsword. He'd taken off his coat; over his shirt he'd draped a tunic that was also a sort of banner, called a *jupon*, front and back: a red Christian cross on a white backdrop.

"A crusader!" the Gnasher hooted gleefully, gnashing his teeth loudly. The Tailpipe was too big for the hall but somehow oozed into the room like lava, behind the Gnasher, who struck an elegant pose, and swung his genitals like a zoot-suit chain. **"What a delight! And with a sword! I'm almost disappointed you can't slay me like Saint...who was it? Saint Someone."**

This last was addressed to Paymenz, who was murmuring something that might have been an incantation, and might have been a prayer, in what sounded like Hebrew.

"It was Saint George," Mendel said, and ran toward the Gnasher, shouting, " For Saint George! For Jesus, the King! For the King!"

"Oh for Christ's sake," I heard the Gnasher mutter.

Then the sword whistled down, cleaving the demon to its groin, like some mighty blow in an Arthurian saga—but the wound sealed up behind the slash. The demon smiling sadly as it healed itself, almost disappointed. It gripped

Mendel's wrist, crushing, making him fall to his knees with pain.

"Run, you imbeciles!" Mendel shouted, as the Gnasher with its free hand wrenched the sword from Mendel and its own gut, drew the sword as casually as from a scabbard...

Paymenz stalked toward the demons, incanting louder, raising his hand. The Gnasher laughed in Paymenz face and ignored him, turned the sword on Mendel, gutting him like a chicken. Paymenz raised his voice and was almost in the Gnasher's reach, as Melissa screamed, "No Daddy!" and I strained to hold her back as she tried to run to him.

Nyerza strode up and struck Paymenz on the back of the neck, so that Paymenz buckled.

"You must take care of the girl, and the Gold in the Urn, Israel!" Nyerza shouted to Paymenz as he dragged him back a few steps. Then Nyerza lifted Paymenz, threw him clear— even as the leviathan tail of the steaming, oozing black Tailpipe lifted and slammed at him. Nyerza dodged aside, was hit glancingly, so that he was spun back, away from the demons, to fetch up against the wall, dazed but uninjured.

The Gnasher had flayed Mendel open, so that blood spread in a widening pool. Mendel was quivering but his eyes were empty; he was dead or in shock. The Gnasher seemed to be probing for something in Mendel's in-sides...with his hands, with his sword, with his mouth, searching more and more frantically through Mendel's wet wreckage. **Where is it? Where!**" Its fury making its voice resonate through my head. ***The Spark! Where!***" After that it raged in the language we called Tartaran: the language of demons. But a baseline meaning was conveyed: Rage, pent-up seeking, frustrated hunger. The Gnasher stepped back from the body and roared—

As if expressing the Gnasher's frustration by proxy the Tailpipe raised its tail and smacked down on Mendel's body, so that bone ends ripped into pinkwhite view and teeth rattled from a shattered jaw.

Melissa swayed, her mouth dropped open. She whimpered. I only *felt* like doing those things.

The Gnasher took a step toward us...Paymenz stepped in front of me and Melissa...Nyerza got to his feet...

Suddenly Mendel was there, intact, apparently alive, as we'd last seen him. But somehow I knew that it wasn't his body I was seeing. "Here is the spark you seek," he said, though his mouth didn't open.

The Gnasher turned to him and slashed with curving talons—which went through Mendel, as if through a hologram. Mendel smiled distantly.

"You cannot harm me thus," said Mendel. "What you call my spark is a flame, and it burns in the realm of All Suns, where you cannot reach it."

Mendel turned to Nyerza and said, "Use the Gold as a shield."

Then Mendel was gone; it wasn't as if he blinked out, it was more like the passing of a memory.

The Gnasher bellowed, **"One spark gone, these remain, calling to their inheritor! Purchase ye my insurance, one payment only! Live forever within me and immediately cash in your premiums! We are a full-service organization!"** And it strode toward us.

"There has to be a back way out!" I said, backpedaling, dragging Melissa with me.

Nyerza shook his head. "They will pursue: the only way out is through."

So saying, he took Melissa by the wrist and swung her in front of him...

And pushed her toward the demons.

I shouted something, I don't know what it was, and ran after her to pull her back, as the Gnasher opened its great jaws to snap at her head, and then felt Paymenz and Nyerza gripping me, each taking an arm. Melissa put her hands in front of her face—

The Gnasher stepped toward her—

Then there was an effulgence. No, a scintillation, a sparkle from just in front of Melissa—issuing from the area of her sternum, I saw, now: quite literally a sparkling, a slowly turning ball of sparkle, each 'spark' big as my hand, the whole growing as it emerged, stabilizing at the size of a bushel; a grand, turning sparkle of gold and violet and electric-blue, but with the gold predominating, giving off a keening sound so high-pitched you couldn't quite hear it, and yet you felt it in your joints. Slowly turning, the orb of unfading sparks hung in the air between Melissa—who seemed in a trance—and the Gnasher…

Who reached for it…

And then recoiled, the demon whimpering so pathetically I wanted to say, *There, there…*

The wheeling ball of sparks moved toward the demons, seeming to draw Melissa like a sleepwalker behind it, and the Gnasher wailed in his own language and clawed its way up onto the steaming black bulk of the Tailpipe, as if taking comfort there, and then scrambled back away from Melissa. The great quivering, steaming, many-mouthed eel-skin flank of the Tailpipe still barred our way, as we stumbled after her, but then the Tailpipe oozed itself into two parts, a kind of macroscopic mitosis, one part splitting off to the right, the other to the left, like the Red Sea in the Moses story, and there was a clear path between the quivering ends of its bifurcation, and we hurried between, through the oily stink of it, and up the ramp, past headless bodies and to the stairs. I turned to see it flow seamlessly together behind us, and it commenced to follow, until the Gnasher shouted something in Tartaran, and it held back.

"This way," Nyerza said. "We go to the helicopter."

I looked at Melissa; the globe of incandescence had vanished; receded into her. She stared into space, listening, with tears in her eyes, as Paymenz whispered something to her.

"Okay," I said. "A helicopter. That's fine. I'll go for that. Sure. Let's do that."

Paymenz held Melissa in his arms, at the back of the chopper; I sat near the front, behind the pilot's seat. The pilot was a dour, stooped gray-haired black man in a paramilitary uniform without markings: one Mimbala, whom Nyerza said had once been an Army Chief of Staff for some African country. Mimbala had started the chopper and left it running in some kind of idle, gone to consult with a spindly white man from the FAA who was trying to provide a strategy for flying safely past the drifting Spiders; the darting Sharkadians. We could see them, instead of airplanes, speckling the sky, here and there, in the distance. Our chopper's blades were chuffing so slowly I could have hung onto them and swung round, like a child at play, and I had an impulse to do just that; to do something meaningless, mischievous, anything to deny the darkness pulling at our hearts like G-force tugging an astronaut who realizes his shuttle won't make it into orbit. Like the astronaut, I wanted to take to the sky.

Mostly to keep my mind busy, I began to question Nyerza.

"The thing that came from her...that drove them back...that saved us...It was—the 'Gold in the urn' that Mendel mentioned?"

"Yes. It needs a human being, to be the urn, the repository, for a time. We planted it in Melissa…"

"Is that…is that what you were doing with her, the other night?" I asked, leaning toward him so Melissa wouldn't hear, my voice as soft as possible over the humming of the idling engine, the chuffing of the rotors.

He looked at me in frowning puzzlement. "No. That, the other night—that was…just a man and a woman. Spontaneous, as you say."

"Not a ritual?"

"No. It was quite natural." He looked out the window, signaled to the pilot—Mimbala raised a hand, palm outward, to say wait a moment. Nyerza turned back to me, sighing. "I will miss having Mendel physically near. The urn…the Gold…This is—what the demons call 'sparks', the being-force of many lives, who're consolidated, in this case, to one purpose. They meditate together, and this keeps them together. They are like…in some cultures they are called Bodhisattvas. The awakened, who return to help us. When we realized that the catastrophe was coming—though we did not know what form it would take—we consulted with these beings, these Ascended Masters, and asked for their help, in its most powerful form: the Gold in the urn. But it needed to be kept in one place, and protected. A few years ago, Melissa was selected as the bearer, the urn…"

"She knew this?"

"She did not. I'm embarrassed to say it was done without her knowledge, as she slept. But this was done with the cooperation of her father. Harmlessly and painlessly."

"A few years ago…"

I remembered, Melissa had been depressed, gloomy, much more into the goth thing. Writing bleak songs like the one the demon had mocked her with. Then she'd changed—

almost overnight. Becoming more centered; more confident; optimistic.

"The 'Gold'…It possessed her?"

"Not at all. It only rode there, in her. But there has been some influence on her, I have no doubt. Its radiance would have been felt, though they try to keep themselves secreted deep within. The demon was trying to drive the Gold from her, perhaps, when it recited her song—a song from a time when she was ruled by, as you might say, quiet despair: that thing which, in some people, opens the door for the diabolic."

I thought I should be angry that Melissa had been used this way. But then, "the Gold" seemed to have helped her; and it saved us all today.

"The demons can't hurt her, at all, while the Gold is with her?"

"In time, they will make their own dark orb, and hunt her down—destroy the urn to destroy the Gold—using their own merged darkness to get to her, surely. Or they may use humans to attack her. But this, you are seeing, will take time. How much, we only speculate. A month or six weeks perhaps, Mendel told me…Ah, here comes Mimbala."

Mimbala returned to the chopper, and threw switches, pulled levers, and it thrummed and the rotors swished faster and faster, the world tilted and we angled into the sky…

* *

We are alone, Melissa and I, in the Professor's chilly, dark apartment; alone with restive cats and dead lava lamps. Except Melissa is never alone, even when I've left her in her room. The Gold is with her, though unseen. It is silent, transparent; it is singing and scintillating: all of these.

I finished writing all the foregoing yesterday. Yes it's amazing what people can get used to. We've been here for weeks, since the chopper pilot landed on the roof of the building.

"There's canned food and water stacked floor to ceiling in that back storeroom," Paymenz had shouted, over the throb of the chopper, "—my divinations, you see, led me to stock up: *I* at least took them seriously! Now you may sing hosannas of praise to my foresight!" He grinned; he was trying to make light of his departure.

"Dad—stay with us!" Melissa shouted. "Or take us with you!"

The engine got louder. "Arrangements...they won't come here...Must go with Nyerza...Events are shaped by...various convergences...luminous..." Luminous something. Repercussions, maybe? "We're going to try to locate the..." I couldn't make out the rest. They took off as he shouted, "Back in touch when possible. You are safe if you stay with her, Ira..."

That's not good for my masculine vanity, but it's true: Melissa keeps me safe.

I don't go out, because I could be killed; Melissa doesn't go out because she doesn't want to see anyone killed. And the looters, the gangs, could take her; use her and kill her, as they have with too many others.

The Spiders departed the balcony some time ago. But streamers of black smoke twist up randomly, across the glassy vista of the city.

Depression comes sometimes, like a wolf prowling at the edge of a campfire's light. I throw what fuel I have on the fire.

The first few days we slept most of the time, she in her room, me on the livingroom couch where I could keep an eye on the front door, pretend I was useful as her guardian.

We slumbered away a weighty emotional exhaustion, absorbing, in riotous dreams and dozing depression, all that we'd seen. The demons, the flight through the city, the Gnasher, the flare of sex, the reshaping of paradigms, the brutal killing of Mendel and his triumph, the revelation of the Gold in the Urn...The Gold, the living wheel of burning spirit that possessed Melissa and yet didn't possess her; that seemed to hum in the background, unheard but felt by those feeling parts of us that are usually dormant.

What people can get used to...People managed a routine even at Dachau; they found ways to survive, psychologically—harder than surviving physically.

In Cambodia, in the days of the Khmer Rouge, people adapted to being forced into an insane plan for an anti-intellectual agrarian utopia, a utopia based on mass murder and the destruction of ideas and common sense; masses of people, after seeing their loved ones butchered, forced from the cities onto farms, forced to work 14 hour days, 7 days a week, 365 days a year; to give up all their old culture, their music, their traditions, every single one of their beliefs; to wear black pajamas and nothing else ever; to be slaves to a demented social meme. They adapted; they survived.

Demons invade the world; people find ways to adapt, to get used to the horror.

Is it, really, any worse than the Killing Fields?

But often I felt a craving for the ordinariness that had reigned before the demons; for the very banality I had sometimes railed against. The mindless, childish ubiquity

95

of mass-media and consumerism; the welcome distraction of dealing with traffic and laundry and phone bills. What a relief real banality would be…

We passed the time as we might, making a pact, for the sake of sanity, to leave the TV in a closet, and listen to a radio news show only once a day. After two weeks Melissa asked me to listen to it alone, away from her. She spent the time meditating, every so often muttering in some language she shouldn't know, in the depths of her meditations; in reading, writing feverishly in a journal.

She encouraged me to paint, to draw, with whatever was handy. I felt tense, balled up inside, reluctant to let it out, to express it. But she gently insisted, and came to muse over my drawings, my pen and inks made with all the wrong sorts of pens and inks.

Sometimes, as I drew, I seemed to see, in my mind's eye, a pentagram superimposed over a city I didn't recognize …I reproduced the city as a simplified map, street-lines intertwined with hermetic symbols, and figures of myth.

One night, in the light of battery-operated lanterns, we sat around the living room, trying not to hear the distant sounds of shouting, combat, sirens, and, from far off, the *crump* of what might be a plane crashing. Some nights were worse than others; this was one of the bad nights.

She'd asked me to read to her, anything I wanted. I chose the Sufi poet Rumi. Consciously or unconsciously. I glanced up at her, from time to time, as I read: She was curled sideways in an easy chair, with two cats on the chair with her, nestled in her hollows; she wore a dark purple sari, no shoes. Her feet drawn up onto the cushion; one hand toying with a silver ring on a toe; her eyes hidden by the drape of her hair. She made me ache.

> *"...A lover gambles everything, the self,*
> *the circle around the zero! He or she*
> *cuts and throws it all away.*
> *This is beyond any religion.*
> *Lovers do not require from God any proof,*
> *or any text, nor do they knock on a door*
> *to make sure this is the right street.*
> *They run and they run..."*

I felt her looking at me, then, and glanced up at her, and our eyes met. Her gaze seemed open, as never before. I found myself putting the book aside, and crossing the room to her, bending to kiss her. She lifted her head to receive and return the kiss, and moved aside on the big chair so I could slide in beside her, the cats irritably jumping to the floor and slinking away. Then Melissa eased herself onto my lap, and I drew her into the circle of my arms...We kissed more deeply...My hands found their way to her thighs, and she let them feel upward from there...

Then suddenly I stopped, and looked down at my hand. It was as if there was a cold, bony grip on my wrist, holding it back, though nothing could be seen. Nothing except a blue-gold sparkling, a throbbing shimmer, that never quite exposed itself yet made itself known... Did I see it? It was as if, instead, I felt it, and made some accommodation in the visual part of my brain.

She felt it too, and went pale, looking up at me. "They..."

"They don't want me to. I'm not...while they're there, it has to be...someone like..." It hurt to say it: "Someone like Nyerza..."

I took my hand away from her thigh; the invisible grip went from my wrist. It all seemed so...lawful. So inevitable. We didn't question it.

She laid her head against my shoulder. "But the time will come."

"I don't know if I'll ever be..."

"You might, but that's not what I meant. They won't always be with me. Not in the way they are now."

"If we live."

"Yes. If we live."

"But you'll belong to Nyerza."

After a moment, she said, "No, I don't think so. He's...a great man. But though he knows better, it's difficult for him to think of a woman as his equal. And even when I'm close to him I'm not close to him. And... there was a sense, when he was...was in me...that he was talking to them...like I was the phone booth. I didn't care for it. I should be honored, but..."

"Do they...do they speak to you? Inside?"

"No. Well yes and no. They hide their light so I am not blinded. Sometimes I think I feel...sort of feel them saying something...but I hear no words..."

"Saying...?"

"I don't know how to put it into words."

We said no more that night, and soon she went to bed. I haven't tried, since. But sometimes she takes my hand, or I take hers, and we hold hands; sometimes she comes into the circle of my arms, and we stand quietly in the middle of the room.

* *

In our area, the police are still operating, in a furtive kind of way. Mostly curtailing the gangs of looters, trying to suppress the parades, because there are always deaths, at the parades, or in their wake.

The parades wind through the streets, the paraders clashing garbage can lids, clanking bottles together, chanting, many of them naked and bright with fanciful body paints. How it began, no one seems quite sure. The parades skirt the areas where the demons are roaming, seem to flirt with them, to invite them; they seem to believe, according to a radio report I heard, that if they thus offer themselves up en masse, the participating individuals have a better chance of survival: *Choose from us but choose not me.*

I watched with binoculars, one dusk, as one of these spontaneous parades of the half-mad wended their way clashing and banging and chanting with an elliptical rhythm into the square below the apartment building; I watched as a Dishrag fluttered down from the sky like a wet autumn leaf just broken from the tree, coming down, soon, to tumble across the ground, now like a tumbleweed; but not tumbling at random. It was seeking, and finding, as it closed on one of the paraders. The demon colloquially called a Dishrag is like fuzzy, blotchy gray and blue terry cloth crumpled up into a ball, about ten feet in diameter, capable of partially unfolding to entrap its victims.

The Rag bounced in pursuit of a short, fat man— perhaps picking the easy kill from the herd—as the parade parted for the hunt, the crowd gawping in awe as the demon's bounce became a pounce, knocking the man down from above, closing over him like a sea creature enfolding a fish. The victim's arms and feet protruded from opposite sides of the crumpled, furry ball, and, as it crushed him, squeezing the juice from him, something else was expressed from him, pressed out from unimaginable psychic pressures, a visible emission of his mental battery, a kind of electric-blue discharge of images, key psychological moments sketched on the air; it was something like the smoky shapes I'd seen coming from the victim of the Spiders—but this was like the movement of a light-pen caught in slow time-exposure: the brief, streaky blue-glow outline of the victim with his parents, his mother beating him with a coat hanger, a Priest making him kneel before an altar and then before him, a girl surrendering to him, a college degree handed to him, a car accident where the girl dies—then the light-cartoons faded, as the man's screams became muted. The crowd was parading around the feasting demon, clashing and clanking and chanting rhythmically, some chant I couldn't make out, and now a Sharkadian was darting down from above...

I turned away, wrenched and feeling suddenly claustrophobic. But something else had caught my attention —from the corner of my eye—

I went back to the balcony railing and looked down to see a nondescript bus pull up, men with guns get out below, far below...Men with guns going into our building.

"Oh no," I said.

I think that's what I said. And I went back inside the building.

Shephard's people, maybe. The black magicians had sent mortals, unaffected by the power of the Gold, to take Melissa away.

I had no way to stop them, but maybe I could misdirect them.

*   *

I ran downstairs, got as far as the second floor stairwell landing, before the soldiers burst into the stairwell and surrounded me. There was a gun shoved against the side of my head, one arm twisted behind me. "Let's see your pass," someone growled in my ear.

"I don't have one." I told them I was from Paymenz' apartment, and then wished I'd bit my tongue. Thinking I shouldn't have told them that.

But it turned out to be the right thing to do. They let me go.

I went out into the lobby and saw the front door was ringed by a semicircle of soldiers. None of the other buildings in the area were guarded. Our guardians seemed almost relaxed as they checked a nervous old woman's building pass. Maybe the soldiers were glad to be here, because the demons were afraid of this building: because the Gold was here. Word had gotten around that the demons wouldn't attack the building because they were afraid of Melissa.

Laboring back upstairs—the elevator was broken, of course—I realized that they had been sent here, through Nyerza's government contacts, specifically to guard the building against Shephard's mortal associates. The bus I'd seen had brought relief soldiers for the next watch; they were protecting Melissa, not threatening her.

Then perhaps it was safe to go to the roof...To get *out*, after all these weeks, really outside...

Enjoying the exercise, I climbed to the roof. I wasn't alone up there.

I didn't see them at first, though I heard a tinkling piano from somewhere—there was a little outbuilding containing the elevator engine housing and the top landing for the stairs, and when I came out of it, they were on the other side, behind me. I strolled across the transplas-coated roof to the railing, reveling in the open air but scanning the sky for nearby Sharkadians or Spiders. I wasn't protected, up here. I was too far from Melissa; from those who were called the Gold.

Then they turned up the volume, and I turned at the sound of someone playing an electric piano. It sounded like a perverse take on honky tonk ragtime.

I walked around to the other side of the out-building, following the sound, and found two figures standing at an electric piano, the tall skinny one one-fingering a bass part, the stocky one in the hat tinkling away at an upper register. The electric piano was portable, on folding steel tube legs, battery powered, and sounded fairly close to an acoustic piano. Up here, it sounded lost, plaintive. I took half a dozen steps toward them, before I realized that the guy playing the upper register...the guy wearing patchy jeans and work boots, and a shabby suit-vest unbuttoned over a dirty white t-shirt...

That his clothes had grown on him; were not real clothes; were part of his skin.

His? *Its* skin. The demon seemed to sense me, as I realized this, and though I very much did not want to see its face, the Bugsy snapped its whole body around and showed its face to me, and we both knew I couldn't look away.

A thing projected from its mouth that looked like a smoldering cigarette, and gave off a greasy steam, but the projection wasn't a cigarette but an excrescence, part of its lip, a growth projecting three or four inches out, camouflage complete with a yellow cigarette filter; I had no doubt there would be a brand name on it too—and the 'cigarette' never burned down. The Bugsy's face was ostensibly human, with a stub nose and flat blue eyes that were a tad too wide, and a slack, froggish mouth, and jagged, uneven yellow teeth. Its proportions were not dwarfish—but its hands were, except for the curving talons on them. Its clothes grew from its skin like the shell of a turtle; and there were blotchy red and yellow running sores on the "cloth" of its vest, pants, and on one side of its neck…Bugsys grew different sorts of "clothes" but they all had those sores…

On its head was a hat, a real hat, taken from some human victim probably; a bashed up gray fedora, which had mostly lost its shape.

A Bugsy, I thought: *There is a fucking Bugsy on the roof.*

It had a human companion—as they often did, for a time. They kept pets for awhile, sometimes for a week or more, I'd heard, and then killed them. The human sidekicks were inexplicably oblivious to their fate until close to the end.

The Bugsy's voice was slurred like a drunk's, by turns gutteral and squeaky. "There'sh my man, there'sh my man," the demon said, "here he ish, Robert, you see this guy? Is he a bleshing or what?"

The skinny, ragged human sidekick, a man who might've been thirty, with hollow eyes so red I couldn't make out his natural eye-color, tittered and rubbed his pointed noise with a grime-caked hand. His nails had grown out and begun to curl, as if in grotesque imitation of the Bugsy's talons. "You think he got any dope on him?"

"No, no I don'ta schmell any, Robert, I mean he's a bleshing for you, because I was jushagonna killya, for somepina do, and here he chiz, he'sa like a bleshing from uh-BUUUUUUUUUV! Gorblesh'im!"

Robert laughed hysterically, glancing at the demon sidelong. *What* had it said about just going to kill…?

Hoping to get them to turn their backs again, I said, "I was enjoying the music. Like to hear some more, if you've got anymore in you."

"You wantsa shee what Robert's got in him huh ya?" the demon said, "cigarette" wagging with each syllable. The Bugsy hooked a talon under Robert's chin, so that blood

103

spiraled down the skinny, grimy neck. Lots of little scars, half-healed cuts on Robert where the Bugsy had toyed with him.

Robert giggled, still pinned on the talon, which the Bugsy was absentmindedly digging in like a man vigorously picking his nose. Robert looked at me desperately as if he wanted to say something.

It was useless, I knew, to tell the demon, *No I don't want to see you hurt him.* I wondered how fast the Bugsys ran, how far they could jump.

Could I make it to the door of the building?

I tried to stay calm, forcing myself to breathe evenly. A little rain began to skirl down…to fall, to ease up, to fall again…A scrap of paper blew spiraling by…

I said, "I was hoping for music. I'd just about do anything for live music about now."

"Really! You do anyshing? Thasha what I wanta hear from more ya pepple, mansy, alla mansies don' wanna do this, don' wanna do that, boring tuh kill, boring to keepa company widshem. You do someshin for me firsh…" The cigarette-shaped growth waggling, "…and I'ma playin you a bigshing…there'sh a girl downstairs, I'm a let you live, be the King, the King, the King of the shecrets, if you let my friend here in to talka her jusha little minute…"

"Just lemme talk to her," Robert said. "Just a little minute."

"Certainly…I'll bring her up here," I said. "Just a moment…"

I backed toward the little outbuilding…the door to the stairs…

"No, thatsh not cool, mothuhfuckuh mansie, you lie to me, yuh fuckin'guy, yuh lyin', now we goin' down the hall, you and Robertya goin first, Robert…he…"

And Robert kills her, I thought.

"Oh fuck it," I said, aloud. The rest I only thought: *Just run.*

I half turned to run for the door—the Bugsy let Robert go and crouched, preparing to spring. I'd never make it to the door. Then I remembered something I'd heard...

I turned back, dug in my pocket, came up with a quarter with lint and crumbs stuck to it. I polished it with my thumb, saying, "Hey uh—I'll bet you anything you want I get heads, you get tails."

The Bugsy froze, then straightened, eyes glazing. They're said to have difficulty resisting an opportunity to gamble. They prefer cards, especially stud poker, but the coin-toss seemed to be working. "Shrow it," the demon said.

I tossed the coin, caught it, flipped it, slapped it on my wrist. "Heads!" I announced.

"But ya didn't make a bet!" Robert blurted, blinking.

I realized that Robert reminded me of someone: my Mom's boyfriend, Curtis. Long time ago.

I said: "I bet—I bet our lives, Robert and mine..."

"Shrow it, fuckin shrow it, I takeuh headsish time," the Bugsy hissed, staring at the quarter in my hand, drooling.

"Sure..." I tossed the quarter up—toward a farther corner of the roof. The Bugsy ran for it.

I mouthed: *Run!* at Robert. He only gaped at me, blinking stupidly, tears staring from his eyes.

I sprinted for the door to the stairs...

"No don't, man!" Robert yelled hoarsely. "He..."

The Bugsy made a sound like a furious boar, and, as I ran, it shouted, "I won thatsh tosh!"

"Wait!" Robert yelled. He said nothing else after that —there was only the scream. It was such a piteous cry, I paused at the outbuilding, just around the corner from the door, to look back. Always a mistake, to look back at a demon.

"You don't wanna see whush I gotferya here?" the Bugsy said, "cigarette" bobbing as with one set of talons it held Robert face down, the other claws digging deeply into Robert's back, demonic grip closing firmly over the writhing human's spine. One hand pushing, the other pulling—with a practiced motion, pulling Robert's spine from his body, the whole spine, as from an overcooked fish, though it was still attached to his skull. Until, there, the spine was yanked free, and the Bugsy waved the vertebrae spatteringly at me. "We cud be friendsh, giveya immortality, shecrets, all tha' shit, teach you do shit like thish whatcha shay..." And as it spoke it strode toward me, waving the segmented dripping-red wand of Robert's spine, holding my trapped attention—

I broke free, and ran for the door, for the stairs, and vaulted over the railing, fell twelve feet, maybe more, to the next landing, a painful landing, hearing the unnaturally soft boot-steps on the stairs above me as the demon came after me, seeing the red bony splintery thing flung past my head and down the stairwell...

I was down just ahead of the Bugsy, through a doorway, down the hall, running to Paymenz' apartment door. With terror-focused concentration putting the key *very exactly right into the lock*, no wasted motions as I inserted, turned the key, got the door open, removed the key and ran in, slammed the door, shouting for Melissa, feeling like such a goddamn little boy, calling for the protection of his mother...

But when she came to the living room, put her hand on the door, I heard, almost immediately, the hasty retreat of the Bugsy padding away down the hall outside...

A little later we heard a rustling outside the window, and saw a Sharkadian flying the Bugsy down from the roof in its arms...The two of them pausing to look toward us, about fifty feet past the balcony railing, hovering to stare before flapping awkwardly away.

* *

The day after the Bugsy, with radical foolhardiness, I decided to visit some kids I'd been giving art lessons to. The soldiers wouldn't accompany me. I got there without running into the gangs. On the way I saw the things I described near the opening of this narrative. The Grindum, the man in the Volvo, and me on my way to teach an art lesson.

On the way home I had to dodge a van full of drunken, glue-sniffing Kid Fundies. Gangs of hysterical teens who think they're supposed to bring about the Final Judgement by punishing the enemies of God, which is whoever they happen on when they're out on the town. Half the time, happily, the demons get them. They nearly ran me down but I cut through a burned-out Tofu Chef place and lost them in the alley.

Since then, been some days of quiet. A Lull. I think it's a Monday afternoon. It's dull gray outside, like a Monday afternoon should be, anyway. The only noise the occasional gunshot. The looters, I guess. Shot on sight, lately.

Quiet. But Melissa and I can both feel it: the imminence. Something is about to happen. Meanwhile, she's meditating in her room and I'm wondering if I'm

—Hold on, there's a pounding at the door. Someone pounding. Going to check it out.

Why don't we have a fucking gun here?! Going...

* *

I'm back; I washed out my mouth but still taste vomit. My hands are shaking. Hard to write.

When I went to the living room Melissa was opening the door—why, I don't know. Stupid to open the door, though the metal door-chain was across the gap.

Standing in the hall was a young guy in a dayglow orange VR-connect jumpsuit, the kind with all those little jacks on them, and lots of peeling stickers from software companies slapped on in between the jacks. The VR doesn't work very well and when they use it they look like idiots, walking on their squirrely little treadmills, and if they aren't real careful the goggles get disconnected or the wires pulled out of the suit. VR-heads get into it anyway. This VR head was shaved, even his eyebrows shaved; he'd have been rockstar-goodlooking if not for that, with his regular features, his cleft chin and high cheekbones and blue eyes. He seemed clean, and, at first, he seemed sane: he didn't seem like a Bugsy slave. And he wasn't one.

"Do you need food?" Melissa asked. "We have a little to spare. Some canned stuff."

"I could use some," the guy said. "I live in the building here, you know, just a floor down." He stuck his hand through the door-space.

Melissa made as if to shake it—I pulled her back. He withdrew the hand, grinning pearly white teeth. His manicure was perfect too. "Look—we should stick together, the people in this building. I've got a good wireless internet connection, the very best, if you wanta come and check it out. I do that Clan Collector website. That's mine, you know. My name's Dervin. Just Dervin." He looked at us, at Melissa then me. "You don't know the name?"

"No...The *what* website, did you say?" I asked.

He seemed genuinely surprised. "Clan Collector. You never heard of it? You're kidding! It's the third most popular site in the country. All seven clans of demons are totally represented...even some interviews!" He spoke fast, chattery, clasping his hands again and again to emphasize each statement. "We've got the best graphics showing them from different angles, run-downs on clan-specific styles of killing, the whole thing. Files on all the different worship-cults, chat rooms, fan voting—right now the Gnashers are the most popular. There's a lot of Bugsy fanatics out there though. Me, I think there's something majestic about the Tailpipe…And I think if we could learn the Tartaran terms for the clan types we could give them names that are, you know, like, more fitting, that honor the whole gestalt of that demon type. You know? And I'm working on that."

Melissa and I looked at each other, then at the stranger. "Did you say fans? And…Bugsy fanatics?" She turned to push one of the cats, a fat tabby named Stimpy, away from the door; the cat wanted to get to what he thought would be outside, and he was pacing behind us, staring at the partly open door into the hall.

"Sure. The demons have a major fanbase."

"A fan base?" she said. "But—they're slaughtering us. In huge numbers."

"Well yeah but serial killers had a big fan following, and so did Hitler. Still does. I spoke to a Gnasher online—he said he was a Gnasher and I think he was but that's, you know, controversial in fan circles—um, spoke to him in the chat room, right? And he said Hitler is actually…" He broke off. Chuckled. "You guys are staring at me like I'm nuts but you're really the ones who're out of it. There was a Fox channel special—they have that mobile Fox Channel trans-mitter, on that bus? You know? That uses that satellite info and dodges the demons? They have that show *The Clans* and it's just pure demonophile stuff."

"O-*kayyyy*," I said. "Whatever. We can let you have some canned goods, what you can carry. I know the build-ing's been getting unevenly supplied—there was a raid on the Army convoy or something, and uh…"

"Ahh—actually…?" He was exchanging stares with the tabby cat. "I'd rather have one of your cats. One or two. You have, what, five?"

Melissa tilted her head as she gazed at him, trying to see if he was kidding. "You're joking, right?"

"Um—no. I can trade you all kinds of stuff for a couple of cats. Or as many as you want to give me."

"Food's that hard to get?" I asked. "I just offered…"

"No—it's for sacrifice. I've got an online relationship with that Gnasher—it's online and ongoing. It's safe, online. But to continue the contact, he requires sacrifices, and he'll accept animals."

"No," I said. "Not a chance. Goodbye. Move away from the door or I'll shout for the soldiers."

Then I saw that he was staring at Melissa's chest—I thought, at first, he was staring at her breasts. But his gaze was lower. And he was reaching behind him. *I've got an online relationship with that Gnasher. Online and ongoing.*

"Oh shit," I said. He put his shoulder against the door so we couldn't slam it and he whipped the automatic pistol around to shove it through the opening. "Run, Melissa!" I yelled.

I jerked the wrist of his gun-hand toward me, with one hand, with the other pulling his elbow, pulling him off balance—he instinctively pulled his arm back a little, so the gun tilted up, and I pushed, hard—and Melissa helped me, ignoring my glare—and the gunmuzzle went back as the gun went off pointing into Dervin's right eye-socket, blowing his eye back into his skull, his brains out through the top of his head in a sudden, brief, thick-red fountain…

We threw his body off the balcony. I don't expect anyone will come and ask about it.

Then I had to run to the bathroom, to vomit, as Melissa knelt by me, sobbing softly, and stroking my hair.

I'm going to go brush my teeth again. At least my hands have stopped shaking.

*   *

In Spring 1987, I came home from school to find our television taken apart, all over the living room floor, and my Mom and her boyfriend, Curtis, crouched tweaking amidst the parts.

"I know what you think," she said, grinning. So cranked up it was an involuntary grin. I saw she'd lost a couple more teeth.

I snorted and tried to ignore them, skirting the wreckage of the TV, the tools they'd used to take it apart; trying to escape upstairs. Curtis was glaring at me; jaws working, grinding—like a Gnasher, it seems to me now. There was a buzzing in his deep hollowed eyes, a vein throbbing on his forehead. (Yeah, the Bugsy's doomed pet, Robert, looked like Curtis; except Curtis was somewhat cleaner.)

"You got a problem, kid?"

"No." I was almost to the stairs. Then I stopped, staring. My boombox. The little portable stereo my aunt had given me. They'd taken it apart. They'd destroyed it. I stared at it, tears in my eyes. It was almost the only thing I owned. I loved music. And they...

"There was a...a bug in it, Curtis found a bug in it," Mom was babbling, "there was a whatdoyoucallit gover-mint gover-mind mind-control controller bug in it, hon, we found it, where is it, I'll show you!"

She scrabbled in the parts and came up with a piece of the CD laser.

"That's for reading CDs," I said, barely audible. "That's not..."

But Curtis heard me. Snarling: "You're saying I'm full of shit?"

I shrugged, dazed, wiping my eyes. "You just…" I wasn't thinking about what I was saying anymore, which was a mistake. "You just do what crank-cases do. You guys are tweaking and you take shit apart and you can't get it back together because you're on a tweaking thing. They all do that. It's a simple inevitability."

Curtis guffawed. "You hear that pretentious shit?" He put on his lame version of an English accent: "It's a 'simple inevitability'!" He stood up, locking his eyes on me.

My mother was feeling the plunge, the crash; slumping where she sat. Her voice was dead as she muttered, "Oh leave him alone, let's put this shit back together…"

"You know why he talks that way the little fucking snot? He studies *art*, he reads Jane fucking Austen! How come? To keep himself separate from us, that's what, to make himself higher, oh he's on a real higher fucking plane, your little prick…"

"I don't know why I'd want to keep separate," I said, wishing I could shut up and run. "Why I wouldn't want to be a crank burn-out, I don't know."

"You little FUCK! What'd you call me!"

After that he was up and hitting me and I was trying to shield myself with my school backpack and he was tearing it from me and *swack*ing me with it, knocking me down, kicking me, cracking my ribs, and then I was scrambling away as my Mom tried to pull him back, babbling something about I was just a kid and didn't understand and forgive him, Curtis, for he knows not what he does, and then he caught me and was dragging me back by the shirttail and I was tearing my shirt to get away from him and running through waves of pain to get to the back door and shouting incoherently and he threw a stereo tweeter at me, it went through

112

the kitchen window, and then he was hitting Mom because she was holding him back and I turned to pull him off her and he hit me, knocked me flat, breaking my nose, and then I heard shouts from the front door...

Some cop had been passing at the corner and a neighbor flagged him down; she'd heard the shouts, seen the window shattering.

Curtis went to jail and did time for assault and possession of a controlled substance, and I went to a foster home, lucked into some pretty nice foster parents, and for two years I focused on doing art that had nothing to do with me or my life and never thinking about anything except what kept me out in front of the pursuer, the dogged pursuit of what it hurts to think about.

Later. 1999. I was out on my own, pretty young, with an art scholarship, and believing that pure art was the only way out of human suffering. Then I heard about my Mom's suicide. Nothing. I felt nothing. I was out in front of feeling anything about it, way out in front and going at a good clip ahead of it...

And then one day I was given an assignment I didn't want, to do some art inspired by a newspaper article, any article. I tried to be inspired by a science article, but nothing came. The only article that seemed to transfer onto the canvas was a long piece about the slave-children of Haiti. Was it December, 1999? I think so. There were, I read, an estimated 200,000 children in Haiti sold into virtual slavery, into indentured servitude and worse, by their parents, sometimes for as little as ten dollars. More often than not the child was given a box in the yard to sleep in; was not allowed to meet the owners' eyes, not permitted to play with other children, not acknowledged at birthdays or Christmas; they were unpaid, underfed, barely clothed oft-beaten servants. It was technically illegal but the authorities in Haiti shrugged and said there was nothing they could do because it was "traditional". I began to draw photo-real images of the children—I began to see *particular* children who, I felt, were not imagined, who really existed, who were actually living in these conditions, often competing with dogs for scraps to eat; working despite having fractured bones, fractures received in beatings...Dying...and replaced by others. And I couldn't sleep—I began to feel them out there, to feel their suffering like a radiation in the air; like heat or a burning UV light. Then I heard about several thousand Albanian prisoners kept in prison by the Serbians even after we'd bombed them into submission, in Kosovo; twelve year old boys crammed in with men, fifty to a room made for eight, forgotten by the diplomats. I could *feel them* there. I read about children in Africa forced to join roaming gangs who called themselves revolutionaries—forced, as initiation, to shoot their own sisters and brothers in the head...I felt their feelings as if they were my own, shared them in waves, transmitted through some unknowable medium...Children in the USA, whose parents were crack addicts, speedfreaks, brutal drunks; children who were taken away from abusive parents and, because there was not enough foster care, were put in juvenile detention lock ups, and forgotten—though they'd committed no crime...I could hear the whimpers, the groans of the suffering in the world—and I heard something else, a sardonic laughter behind it all...I saw the indifference of those who committed these crimes—and I saw the motivation behind that indifference: simple abject selfishness, pure appetite: and I saw, beneath that selfishness, that unfettered appetite, the faces of demons...of demons.... Of demons...

The nervous breakdown was swift in coming. But I was only in the hospital for three months. I quit the medication the day I quit the hospital. I simply learned to plug my ears, to not hear the groan of the world. To deaden myself. To go back to sleep.

I managed it most of the time, anyway. Most of us do. It's a skill you learn.

Then the sky thickened, and the clouds hung heavy, and gave birth to the Seven Clans...

7

Has it been three days, or four? With all that's happened, and happened so fast, and the journey across the various timezones and datelines—I don't know.

A few days ago I woke to hear Melissa talking to someone. It wasn't the way she talked to the cats.

I sprang from bed, afraid there'd been a break-in, found her in the living room—on a cellphone I hadn't seen before. She was looking at a drawing I'd done...done and done and done over again...

"No I think this is it. Come and see it. Now, seriously. Okay." She broke the connection, turned to see me staring at her.

"Where'd you get that phone?"

"Nyerza gave it to me. I just haven't needed it till now. They gave it to me for something specific. We're here about you, as much as anything else, you know. They felt you needed a haven, a familiar place to go to ground for..." She pointed at the drawing. "For this, I think. They're on their way here. I have to meditate. Wait out here, okay?"

"But..."

She wouldn't say anything else, and didn't come out of her room till they arrived four hours later, in the same helicopter they'd left in.

117

Nyerza and Paymenz came into the living room, look-ing around with, I thought, relief. Cluttered and eccentric, but it was a home, even so. I wondered what conditions they'd been living in. Both men looked haggard; Paymenz wore the same clothes I'd last seen him in. He embraced Melissa, shook my hand, greeted the cats, as Nyerza stood at a small wooden table I used for my art, looked at one of my drawings.

"Have you had enough to eat?" Paymenz asked.

"Sure," I said. With the intermittent famines going on, out there, it would've been childish to complain about the quality of the food. We were lucky to eat anything.

There appears to be a corpse on the roof," Paymenz said. "The birds have been at him, so it's hard to tell, but he seems to have been...filleted."

"Yes. There was a Bugsy up there...but—the Bugsy wouldn't come near Melissa. The guy on the roof was supposed to get at her, someway. He failed and..."

"And have there been other human attacks?" Nyerza asked, looking up from the table.

"One. Prompted by some guy's internet contact with the demons, oddly enough."

"Not so odd," Paymenz said, sitting wearily on the arm of the easy chair. "They've been very playful that way." He smiled crookedly. "The Gnashers have developed a real affection for mass media. I expect them to sign with William Morris, soon."

I was pretty sure he was kidding.

Nyerza looked at me and I knew he wanted me to come to stand beside the table. "Yes?"

"This drawing, Ira...Do you, then, know what city this is?"

"I don't, I assume it's an imaginary one."

"No. We have been surveying American cities...this is certainly Detroit. This symbol, here—what does it mean? I have seen it somewhere but that sort of arkana is not my specialty..."

"Astrological symbol of the planet Saturn. I don't know why it's there. It just felt right."

"We will go there, to that part of Detroit—and find out. You have been chosen as an Interpreter. The Solar Soul—the Gold in the Urn—has been guiding you. It resides in Melissa—but sometimes speaks to you. Come—the roof..."

"Wait," Melissa said, with her head cocked, as if she were listening to something only she could hear. "I...think I should bring some broth."

Nyerza looked at her in surprise. "Broth? I can obtain government food supplies. We don't need..."

"Broth. I have some chicken soup in cans. I'll put it in a thermos..."

Paymenz looked at Nyerza and shrugged.

* *

A short, stomach-churningly turbulent trip by helicopter to a private air strip in a Marin County eucalyptus grove; then a tense, smooth trip in a private jet to Detroit. I felt disoriented, shaken, as the trip wore itself away. Melissa simply slept. Paymenz would answer none of my questions. "Let's just see," was all he would say.

A drizzly evening in an armored limosine. The limo drove around abandoned cars on the freeway, around rubble on the street, to a deserted refinery on the edge of Detroit. A Grindum leapt from the trees beside the road, bounded toward us, each leap closer making my heart thud louder. The limo screeched to a halt as the Grindum blocked our way, a hundred feet off. As it stalked snufflingly toward us, Nyerza said, "Hit the accelerator, drive right at it!"

The driver—Mimbala, who'd piloted the chopper—shook his head doubtfully but obeyed. He floored the limo and we roared at the Grindum—and it leapt straight into the air, just before we'd have struck it. I didn't see it come down from the first jump, but a few seconds later saw the demon in the distance, bounding away from us.

I glimpsed the shadow of a Sharkadian ripple over the road's shoulder, as if it were pacing us, some distance overhead; less than a quarter-mile behind, a Spider drifted like Hell's own dandelion puff through the sky, after us. But never coming too close.

Melissa and the Gold in the Urn again...

Paymenz had a flashlight on my drawing; was comparing it to a detailed map of the area. He pointed to a gravel road that led off to the side; there was a chained steel gate in a hurricane-fence blocking the way. "There!"

We'd passed the turn; we had to stop and back up. Mimbala got out and broke the lock with a big iron mallet and chisel from the trunk of the car, and then drove us through.

"Touch nothing," Paymenz said, as we got out of the limo. We stood between empty-looking cinder-block buildings in the shadow of a rusting oil refinery. "This area is blighted—there was an industrial accident here. You remember—almost the same time as the one in Hercules. About twelve hundred people died in the toxic cloud...How much they've cleaned the surroundings, since, I don't know..."

We looked around the dark, nondescript buildings—and then we saw the faintly phosphorescent shape of a man step out from a doorway: It was Mendel. Wearing medievel armor, now, and the *jupon,* red cross on white—gesturing for us to come.

He turned and vanished into the closed door. We hurried to the door, and found it doublelocked. Mimbala and his chisel again, a prolonged, painfully-loud pounding with the mallet, that echoed off the deserted buildings around us—I was sure the dissonant ringing would bring someone, or something. But no one came.

Then he had the door open and we went in; there was a grudging, dim yellow light over a stairway that led underground...

Deep underground. Ten flights down, another door opened into a sort of antechamber within which was a stone structure: a *mastaba* of some reddish stone—but it had been built recently: a reproduction of a low, slope-sided, oblong structure used as an entrance to certain Egyptian tombs. There were Egyptian gods painted on the front in the hieroglyph style—on one side of the door, an image of Set. On the other—

"I don't recognize that one," I said.

"Aumaunet," said Melissa. "Mistress of infinity."

"And there—" I pointed at other symbols. "Hermetic symbols, pentagrams, symbols from the Kaballah—they don't belong with Egyptian images. They've mixed all the symbology up..."

"It's not mixed up, exactly," Paymenz said. "They're symbols from various cultures but meaning the same thing. And what is symbolized in iconography is repeated, here, in text." He pointed to an inscription over the door, likely the same statement repeated in various languages, and in hieroglyphs. "I think that one is Sumerian...and here, I can read this one—in ancient Greek. It refers to a simple exchange: *To the dark god, we give life; from the dark god, we receive life.*"

Nyerza seemed impatient with the *mastaba*. He gestured, and Mimbala, increasingly nervous, set about opening this last door, which was made of gnarled black wood.

A few strokes of the chisel, and the dark wooden door swung inward, onto a short flight of stone steps, leading to a brief concrete corridor, and another door, of blue painted metal, lit by an overhead bulb. This door was unlocked, and opened onto a vast subterranean chamber—a room big as a football field.

We stepped inside, trying to take it all in. The room was awash in the harsh glare of fluorescent strip-lights on a ceiling so low Nyerza had to stoop. Under the lights were hundreds of portable hospital beds; on each one, a recumbent figure, a man or woman, to all appearances dead. They wore ordinary street clothes; their skin seemed grayish, and there were cobwebs on some of them. But they did not seem to be in a state of decay. From somewhere came the hum of powerful ventilation fans, the whisper of an artificial breeze.

"These people," Melissa said. "They're so…they seem so still…Are they dead?"

"I do not believe so," Nyerza said. "They are asleep and beyond asleep—in a state of suspended animation of some sort. Almost that catatonia which mimics death…"

"A vast premature burial," Paymenz murmured. "Poe would be most distressed to be here."

Melissa gasped softly, grabbed my arm, and pointed: and I saw Mendel, in the center of the room, head bowed in prayer. An apparition, he was there but not there. His form ever-so-slightly transparent.

"Oh thank God you've come," came a croak from someone else in the shadows to my right.

Shephard limped into view, shuffling painfully to within a dozen steps of us. I barely recognized him. His suit was in tatters; he wore a ragged beard streaked with what might have been old vomit, and dried blood; his eyes flickered in deep sockets. He seemed bent; his clothes hung on him so loosely, a shrug might've dropped them to the floor.

"Stop there," Paymenz said, drawing a small automatic pistol from a side pocket.

Melissa looked at the gun and her father in surprise.

"I think it is all right," Nyerza said. "Or—all right for now. I do not believe he can hurt us."

"Nor would I," wheezed Shephard. "This place is supposed to be demonically protected. There are dozens of them, all seven of the clans, roundabout the building's exterior. Yet...yet you have entered unmolested. The Gold in the Urn must indeed be here, with you...Yes?" He looked at Melissa. I saw her squirm a little under his febrile gaze. "But yes, yes...inevitably yes..."

"Why are you here now—and not entranced?" Paymenz asked, looking around for Mendel. The apparition was no longer visible.

Shephard licked his cracked lips. All his former insularity, his machine-like poise was gone. He seemed a shell, sustained by will alone. "I...." He shook his head, unable to speak for a moment, coughing, covering his mouth with bony fingers.

"Sit down, Professor Shephard," Melissa said. "Rest yourself." Adding to herself: "Now I know who the broth is for..."

She'd been carrying the thermos in a big leather purse, looped over her shoulder. She knelt beside Shephard and helped him to sit up, giving him a red-plastic thermos cup of broth, and then another, bit by bit. He drank it eagerly. She had to restrain him, at times, so he didn't overdo it.

At last he pushed her hand away. "God bless you, my dear."

"God's name is defiled on your lips, Shephard," Nyerza rumbled.

"Yes," Shephard said, looking sleepy now. "Yes, perhaps. I do not intend defilement. I ask forgiveness—and I have suffered, Doctor Nyerza, for the sake of my penance, yes suffered before God, these many weeks, in this very room. I brought a little food and water with me, but it was not enough. And I was sick, for so long…so sick….And the visions…the terrible visions…But you see…I was sure the Gold in the Urn would come, if only I could survive a day longer, an hour longer…a minute longer…And so it proved. I thought I heard Mendel whispering to me. Dear Mendel, whom I hated—yes, hated!—at one time." He laughed sadly. "Oh how deep is my fatigue, deep and cold as the …long since I could sleep…How I have envied *their* sleep…And feared it, too…"

He seemed to droop, but straightened a little as Paymenz moved to stand over him. "You will not sleep," Paymenz said, his voice hypnotically commanding. "But you will tell us what takes place here, and your part in it."

"I was…was to be one of these," Shephard said, pointing at the hundreds in the vast room suspended in the sleep that mocked death. "I was to be in the final group. The Ushers, we were called, preparing the way, enacting the final rituals. But then—then I saw what became of the world …And in the eyes of the demons I beheld a mirror. And in that mirror I saw my soul. And I crumbled, and it all fell apart for me…I came here—to try to wake them, and could not. I sensed that if I left—the Tartarans would destroy me, and suck my pitiful little spark away. May I have a little water?"

Paymenz shook his head and opened his mouth to deny the water; but Melissa said, "Quiet, Daddy. And put that gun away."

She took a little plastic container of bottled water from her purse, and helped Shephard drink a little of it. He wiped his lips and patted her hand. "Thank you. And those who accompany you...I thank them...I thank all who..."

"Speak!" Nyerza said. "Finish your story!"

Shephard hugged his knees to him, and, in a cracked voice, went on, "There are not so many demons as people think, but many re-appearing, helter skelter. There are a few thousand, sometimes bi-locating. Even one can be terribly destructive, of course. They are...also these." He pointed at the sleepers. "They are possessing the demons."

"You mean—the demons are possessing them in some way?" I asked.

"No, Ira...They possess the demons. The demons in their own world are just...complex appetites, minimally self-aware creations—almost like Artificial Intelligences, but of a spiritual variety. Self aware and yet..." He paused to swallow, to gather his strength. "...And yet not self aware. Living, to some extent sentient, but not imbued with soul. They are the...the side effects of humanity at its worse—the psychic consequence of our cruelties, our self-ishness, our brutality, echoing in the planes of metaphysical creation, finding its own level. Not Hell, not Sheol—that is just the sunless absence of God—but a world that parodies our world at its worst. There are many more than Seven Clans, of course. Only Seven have come so far—but more will come, oh yes, when they're through: this I have seen..."

Paymenz and Melissa looked questioningly at Nyerza.

"Yes," Nyerza said. "More will come unless these are stopped. Speak on, Shephard."

"If I must...The Tartarans are long-lived but in a way more temporary than humanity—the root-souls of human beings are eternal, you see. Certain practitioners of ritual magic, early in the last century, came into sufficient consciousness to create *real* magick. With this…with only this stupid little magickal tool… they sought to secure immortality for themselves—to remake the rules…To achieve not only immortality but a state of what they believed would be godhood—each would, they hoped, become the ruler of some personal cosmic realm. As of old, this called for human sacrifice—but vast numbers of sacrifices were needed. Thousands, thousands, thousands of deaths—and there were two methods; many could be killed, *all together*…or…many could die over time as the result of a deliberate act: and by a kind of slow poisoning. You see?"

"Not…well, not entirely," I said.

He gestured as if waving a fly away from his face. "A mass human sacrifice that in some cases came about in minutes—as in Bhopal, as in Hercules, as here, in this half forgotten little suburb of Detroit. Or, in other cases—other ceremonies—the sacrifices came about over a generation or two. Slow, roasting cancerous death in the 'cancer corridors' of Louisiana, in other places in this country, in other countries…In rooms like this one, men and women chanted, and carried out their ceremonies, as those around them died. Sometimes the entire rite took place in one night; sometimes the ceremonies were repeated at the Solstices …When environmental regulations in some countries tightened up, they resorted more and more to industrial 'accidents'…" He chuckled. A miserable sound. "That Certain One, with whom such deals are struck—*he* told them how to carry this out. Eventually it became obvious that industrial pollution caused cancer, emphysema, and so forth. Yet the industries denied and denied and covered up…for many decades they did so…They did not care. Some were simply blinded by greed and indifference—yet that fed the demonic too, of course. Others worked actively for the Brotherhood…and set up the sacrifices quite deliberately, oh my yes. It was all for the greater good—that some human beings, at least, would become 'like gods'...so they told themselves. So I told myself. The sacrifices were acceptable losses. Like Roosevelt's sacrifice of Pearl Harbor, to galvanize the country into a war—like Hiroshima to end the war. Acceptable losses of life for something great..."

"And you believed this—about it being acceptable?" Melissa asked gently.

Shephard nodded mechanically. "I did. I was the great rationalizer, always. Until forced into...a kind of involuntary *vigil* here...in this great ugly sensory deprivation tank of a room...and inevitably I could not help but see myself as I was...see my colleagues in conspiracy as they are..."

"The actual mechanics of all this?" Nyerza prompted. "Anything more?"

"Yes...a little water... yes the...the industrial areas—those 'industrial parks' and factories involved in the sacrifices—were not...were not laid out at random, oh no, my good friends no..."

Nyerza seemed to grind his teeth at the term of endearment coming from this man, but kept his silence, as Shephard, after sipping water, went on:

"...Each 'ISZ' as we called it..."

"An acronym for what exactly?" Paymenz asked sharply.

"'ISZ'? Oh yes of course—*Industrial Sacrifice Zone.* The *Primary* ISZ's are where the sleepers are found, now, all underground. Here you'll find those who did the deed at Hercules, other places, as well as Detroit. Each ISZ was laid out in the shape of a particular rune—seven runes in all, you see. Even...even the shapes of the oil refineries, certain other mills...those at the ISZ's...were adapted from their necessary shape, in the science of refining...so that against the horizon they etched runes in the Seven Names..."

Nyerza and Paymenz exchanged startled glances. I thought I saw a flicker of admiration in Paymenz's eyes as he looked at Shephard, then. Paymenz murmured, "The scale of the undertaking...astounding...almost majestic."

Nyerza threw Paymenz a pantherish look of warning.

"But..." I said, waving a hand at the tranced figures on the multitude of gurneys. "But the trance...the sleep. They..."

"It was supposed to be temporary. It was supposed to be over, weeks ago. Occupying the demons, they were to take many souls, many sparks from the Pleroma—to consume them for the second half of the undertaking, the transfiguration into gods. But...It never came about. That Certain One Who Cannot Be Named spoke just once when we ventured to inquire. It said...we have argued what it said...but it was something like, *A promise to men is in the words men use; such words have no single meaning...Words mean what I say they mean...*" He broke off, and began to sway to and fro, cackling to himself. "Yes, we ventured to inquire! Heeeee-uh-heee...we ventured...we ventured to..."

"Stop it!" Nyerza growled, hunkering near him, so that Shephard slunk back, scrambling clumsily away on the concrete floor.

"Don't hurt me! I've been through enough! Or just... oh, simply cut my throat. But don't hector me...I am a house of cards, inside! I'm going to need therapy and...and medication!"

"Stop whining and answer! How may we waken these sleepers? How may we end the demonic attack?"

Shephard clutched himself, and tittered sourly. "You have just said it: you end the demonic attack by waking the sleepers! They are just the extrapolation of all mankind. Men sleep *even when they think they are awake*—the true

128

Self sleeps—and because it sleeps we are ruled by the egoic, by vanity…by the *demonic*. Unchecked, unchanneled, it rages where it will! Sometimes in quiet cunning, friends, dear friends—sometimes in overt brutality! Even those… those of us who managed some higher consciousness—it's in all the wrong parts of us! We're all…we're like…like the Elephant Man—all overgrown in the wrong places, inside…"

"How can they be awakened, Professor?" Melissa asked more gently.

"But I don't know! If I knew—I'd have done it! I came here with drugs, various drugs, to awaken them, and I administered them…Nothing worked. I used those drugs to keep myself awake, for weeks at a time, for fear I might become like them…You see before you the result—I am a wreckage…But these…these sleepers cannot be awakened by any ordinary medical means—no, nor by icewater — nor by blasting symphonies in their ears!"

"And if you kill them—you render the demons permanent, or so I suspect," Paymenz murmured.

"Yes. They are what they are. As the sleepers sleep, *each has a corresponding demon, who rages in the outer world.* And how the demons look, what they do, is partly sustained by what the path the sleepers chose, by their acts—but also by the sleep of the rest of humanity! If the human race—even some great portion of itself—saw itself as it was, there would be a…a ripple effect…that would be some help." As he went on he slowly slumped into a fetal shape, lying on his side, muttering, the words more and more difficult to hear: "But the *shock* required to wake those who sleep this sleep…Well, it's too late to be self generated by the sleeper. Such a shock comes only from…from a kind of grace coming from something greater than all of us…from the Solar level, the next higher plane…But how, how to…to focus that, to…I don't know…I thought perhaps…I don't know…" He shook his whole body, as he might have once shaken only his head, and fell silent… And then he went limp.

We looked at him, at one another; back at Shephard. I asked, "Is he dead? Asleep?"

Melissa touched his neck. After a moment she shook her head. "Neither. Unconscious." She stood, and looked at the sleeping multitude. "Or in a trance of some kind. Perhaps he has become like one of these others…"

"No," Nyerza said. "Not yet."

"Mendel was here," I said. "He must intend…something. You who are…You in the circle. Didn't you know about all this?"

Nyerza gazed at the sleepers and mused, "We knew almost nothing of all this…because they had suffused the world in distractions, and darkened the world with media, with wave after wave of their dark suggestions…We knew they were hiding something—but we guessed at nothing so vast." Then he added, "Then again, some guessed. And they were not listened to."

"Yes," Paymenz said. "Mendel suggested something of the sort. So I've heard. We knew the Brotherhood of That Certain One were using some aspects of industrial civilization for evil—but the obvious evil blinded us to the subtle, the Great Plan…We thought it was all for the sake of chaos, to keep humanity off balance, easy to prey on. But that was only half of it…And even now—the waves of darkness hide the truth—even from the Ascended Masters…"

"No longer," said Mendel. His voice resonated with that unnatural, psychic vibrancy the Gnashers sometimes had. But where the Gnasher's tones had radiated impulses to self doubt, to raw fear, Mendel's voice gave hope, and subtle energy.

We saw him again, standing amidst the sleeping multitude...

**"We now see what needs be done. Only one
more was needed—myself—to add to the
noospheric energy, to dispel the darkness. Follow
the woman, one sleeper to the next. Be guided by
her."**

With that he was gone. And Melissa drew her breath
in sharply. She touched her solar plexus, and shivered.

* *

We followed her. From one sleeping figure to the next.

They were all adults, of every possible adult age, of
every type, of every race—though there were perhaps more
middle-aged white males than any other single type.

As Melissa came to the first sleeper, the Gold in the Urn
emerged from her—resplendent.

She quivered, her knees buckling, as it came fulminat-
ing, sparkling and shining from her; a sidereal birth pang that
left her shaking, gazing with parted lips, with eyes reflecting
the shimmer...

"This...this Golden thing," I murmured to Paymenz.
"Could it—awaken me? Could she use it to...to make me—
enlightened?"

"No—enlightenment, and the states of consciousness
beyond enlightenment—the recognition of True Essence in
oneself, the creation of real Being—these things must be
earned. They must be paid for. By personal effort, by
conscious suffering. What will happen here is only a return
to ordinary consciousness—and I suspect the Gold will show
them one thing more..."

She turned to Mimbala, and in a voice that wasn't quite hers, said, "Go there—to the box on the wall. Shut off the false light."

He looked at Nyerza, who nodded. Mimbala trotted to the power box, and threw the switch. We were dropped into a vast well of darkness—which was immediately abated in a hemisphere of light around us— the light of the Gold.

Then she put out her right hand, palm upward, and the shimmering orb floated to suspend the core of itself six inches over her palm, so that its energies all but hid her hand from view, and lit up her body...And lit her face and eyes from beneath...blue and gold...

She moved her arm to the nearest of the sleepers, a young man, and lowered her hand so that the energies suspended over her palm swept over the sleeper's head, and almost instantly, he awoke.

He awoke with a wrenching cry of authentic agony. That is the only possible word for the sound that came out of him: *agony*. A cry of agony.

We were to hear that sound repeated hundreds of times, as we passed from one recumbent figure to the next.

The awakened seemed inconsolable, though some drifted into groups, here and there, and clutched one another for comfort, weeping without articulation; others crept under their gurneys and hugged themselves, crying, quivering with horror, eyes wide, staring around; yet looking, somehow, inward—

Seeing themselves, through the power of the Gold in the Urn, as they really were.

There were many cries of agony.

We found out later...

...that a seven-year-old Hispanic boy and his young mother were making their way on foot to a government emergency food distribution center, through city-issued routes that were supposed to be 'behind the demonic wave', when a flying Sharkadian, carrying a Bugsy, spotted them crossing a street.

I don't know if the Bugsy was "my" Bugsy, but it came to them the way it had left us. The Sharkadian lowered the Bugsy on one side of the terrified mother and son, then flapped to obstruct their escape down the rubbled street.

The young mother whispered to her son: *Run, when I give the signal.*

The Bugsy told her that she should tell him, instead, to run right to the Sharkadian. It'd be over faster that way. Unless the Bugsy itself decided to take the boy as his "li'l pal". The Bugsy said it hadn't had a "li'l pal" quite that little before. But perhaps the lady would like to dance, first. The two of us, said the Bugsy—a polka, perhaps.

"If I dance, if I do whatever you want, you let my son go?"

Depends, said the Bugsy, what you mean by let him go.

Then the Sharkadian, impatient, leapt forward, clapped its talons onto the Mother's shoulders, opened its jaws so to snap her head away, as the child screamed...

"That's when the one who had me was pulled away from me," the mother said, later. "Like something had him by the tail and was pulling him. I don't know why he couldn't pull me with him, it was like he had no strength in him then."

The Bugsy gave a whimpering cry and tried to crawl under a car, but it did no good: the same thing was happening to the Bugsy as happened to the Sharkadian. The demons began to *fall away into themselves.*

We've heard the description again and again, by now, and always more or less the same: The demon was like something receding into the distance at great speed—as if you'd dropped the demon, any of the seven clans, off the roof of the World Trade Center, and watched from up there, watched it falling away from you, shrinking with its going. Only, it was falling into itself, somehow, *into the centerpoint of where it had been.* It vanished into the distance— without moving an inch.

The boy and his mother clutched one another and watched as the two demons shrank into nothingness and were gone. Mother and child fell to their knees and thanked God and went safely home.

The story was told again and again, in thousands of places, across the world...

And each vanished demon corresponds to a human being, a conspirator of the Brotherhood of That Certain One, awakened by my own darling Melissa and the Gold in the Urn. Exactly when the demon's corresponding human woke, the demon was hurled back into its own plane, back to where it was and wasn't, and that which made it possible to inhabit our world returned to its originator, and woke them to an agony of self-knowledge...

As Melissa finished waking the sleepers at the first ISZ, Nyerza switched the overhead lights back on, and she turned to see Nyerza's man, Mimbala, pointing a gun at Shephard's head.

Shephard was on his hands and knees, weeping, crawling toward her, across the room.

"Dr. Nyerza!" Melissa shouted.

Mimbala cocked the gun...

"Mimbala will not pull that trigger!" Melissa bellowed.

Nyerza looked at her. She'd raised her voice to a loudness I'd never have thought possible. "You will let that man be!"

She strode toward them, and as if in retreat from her anger, the Gold in the Urn now vanished within her, for a time.

Mimbala fired the gun.

Most of Shephard's left ear disappeared. There was a red smear down his neck and he clutched his head and rocked in pain.

Mimbala's old hands were shaking. He steadied his right hand with his left—

Melissa came to stand a few yards away. Mimbala hesitated—looking at her, and then Nyerza. But keeping the gun extended; aimed at the cowering Shephard.

Melissa spoke in a gentler tone. "Nyerza—? Please. Leave him be."

"Let them kill me," Shephard said hoarsely.

"No," Melissa said. "Nyerza—?"

"He's one of them—and soon," Nyerza added, "he will be a sleeper, like those you've awakened. He is lying to us about his intentions—perhaps misleading us completely about everything."

"No," she said. "I don't think so."

She looked at me, and I sighed and walked over to stand beside her.

"So you can be Conscious, Nyerza—and without compassion?" I asked.

"I can kill if absolutely necessary," said Nyerza. "I believe that if we let this man live, he will become like these others—when we cannot reach him. And another demon will walk the Earth. How many will it kill? To save those people—kill him now."

I turned to Melissa. "Unless—can you wake him now…?"

"No…it doesn't…doesn't feel like it." She looked sharply at Nyerza. "Here's the irony: Some part of *you,* Nyerza, has gone to sleep. Maybe it's the burden you've carried, the last few weeks. No one could bear it. Don't feel bad…But see this impulse to kill Shephard for what it is."

Nyerza opened his mouth as if to speak—then seemed to gaze into space for a moment. Or, into himself.

Paymenz was watching the others, who muttered and groaned and cursed in the room. "I think we'd better make up our minds and leave. Nyerza—she is guided. Trust her."

Mimbala looked at Nyerza questioningly—Nyerza closed his long fingers over Mimbala's wrist, and shook his head.

"Let him be," Nyerza said, reluctantly. "She is right…"

Melissa strode up to them, skirts swishing.

"Shephard will come with us," she said.

"This?" Paymenz said, pointing at Shephard. "He is one of them! How many have died because…"

"Daddy—be silent!"

Paymenz fell silent out of sheer astonishment.

She went on, more quietly, and even more authoritatively, "He comes with us. He will lead us to the others."

Shephard required a wheelchair. Nyerza's government contacts provided military helicopters and transport jets normally used only for the Brass, and an Army nurse for Shephard.

We traveled, with snowballing exhaustion, from one Primary ISZ to another, Shephard guiding us. Six more—there were three more Industrial Sacrifice Zones in the USA—one in Louisiana, one in New Jersey; then we skipped to three overseas, flying across the Atlantic; we hopped the globe, traveling, in hours, to Primary ISZs in India, Africa, Malaysia.

Behind us, those forcibly awakened slowly emerged from the vast underground rooms, and fared variously: some retreated into madness; some went into a long depression, and then a sort of amnesia; a fair number committed suicide; some found their way to synagogues, Buddhist temples, churches, mosques, cathedrals, even sweat lodges, to ask intercession and forgiveness; one man crawled forty-three miles on his hands and knees till he was grinding bone ends on concrete, as some sort of inarticulate act of expiation; many simply let their health tumble apart, in alcohol and drugs. And died. They all had this in common: a fear of sleep; a determined sleeplessness.

We crossed the Pacific to the last ISZ—in the Los Angeles area.

They were waiting for us…

…in California. We saw them twenty minutes after we trudged wearily down the ramp into California. Melissa coming down out of the back of the squat plane first, and then the men hiding behind the woman: Nyerza, Paymenz, Nyerza's man Mimbala, myself, Shephard and his nurse, four buddhist Monks, a Sikh teacher, and an Islamic Sufi we'd picked up in India. We emerged blinking in sunlight from the military transport plane we'd appropriated, with the blessing of the Air Force, in Hawaii. The plane had landed on a broad road that led up to the chemicals factory twenty minutes north of the northern edge of the San Fernando Valley. The site of an 'accident'...

We looked up at the ISZ: The factory stood against the yellowish late afternoon sky in a shape that was largely vertical but with pipes and catwalks crossing horizontally, diagonally: the now-obvious silhouette of a giant rune...

But our small group wasn't alone: three trucks of National Guardsmen arrived almost at the same moment, looking pale and frightened. Sent to help us by a Presidential administration encouraged by Melissa's successes. But the Guardsmen had seen many hundreds of their kind torn to pieces in the past months...They seemed very young...Still they climbed dutifully from their trucks, checked the clips on their rifles, gazed pensively around them.

As we approached the side road that led down to the underground chamber of sleepers, I felt a constriction, a chill, seeing long lines of dark figures issuing from the grove of dead oak trees to either side of the road; the leafless, twisted, blackened trees themselves looking like free-hand runes, some fanciful, forgotten script signifying only decay and death.

But those who paraded from the dead woods to block our way were human—most of them. There were, however, three Bugsys, looking almost identical, in the forefront. Milling around the Bugsys were some four hundred men and women, many of them naked but for sandals and garish body paint; painted in ribald imagery, geometric designs, pentagrams; on some were crude pictoglyphs of Spiders and Tailpipes. Others wore papier mache false-heads resembling Gnashers and Grindums and Sharkadians; crude hand-sewn costumes mimicking the demons' shapes.

These were people, I thought, terrified into making their own desperate accommodation with the new—the *apparently* new—demonic reality.

Some carried hunting rifles, pistols, axes, baseball bats and steel pipes...

The National Guardsmen looked almost glad to see them. They could be shot down, dead, and they would stay dead.

A Bugsy stepped forward, with his hand on one man's shoulder, guiding the man toward us like a parent gently urging a child to step forward and recite a poem.

The lanky potbellied man, with a ragged grey-streaked red beard, was almost naked, painted mostly blue, with bands of bright red around his limbs; his genitals bright orange; on his head was a hand-sewn cloth hood that was a sort of pathetic muppet of a Sharkadian. In one hand the man held a staff, made from a long-obsolete television aerial, with bits of mummified human parts dangling from its remaining crossbars: mummified fingers, a string of ears, a whole hand, a man's head—the head mostly just skull, now...

There was a teasing familiarity about the face of the man in the Sharkadian hood, despite the paint and the beard and the gauntness. Wasn't he an important candidate for governor, before the invasion?

I put an arm instinctively around Melissa's shoulders; we heard a snorting, a flapping, glanced up to see Sharkadians wheeling a few hundred feet overhead; to see Spiders drifting in from three directions...

Some of the soldiers whimpered, seeing the demons gather.

"More are coming," said the man in the Sharkadian hood, stepping forward, alone; the Bugsys holding back. The man adopted a low, portentous voice. "Your destruction of the new world will end here."

139

"We destroy nothing," Paymenz said. "We only awaken."

"And what becomes of those you damage with your waking?" the man demanded. "They go mad, they kill themselves..."

"Some do—awakening such people brings them to a particular remorse—one that's hard to bear. They have more to be remorseful about than many others do."

"You are murdering them, with your black magic," the man said, perplexing us all.

"Black magic?" I blurted.

"The angels whom your magic has blighted, has darkened, have been winnowing the human race, removing those whose souls were not pure enough to ascend at the Great Dance to come..."

I had to laugh—maybe it was from a weariness-bred hysteria. "Angels! Is that what they've told you? Winnowing? Purifying? You see them torture and mangle people and you still believe they have some kind of good intentions?"

"We see the distortion your dark magic has brought about!"

I looked at the rest of the parader mob. I saw there were at least fifty who were dressed more or less normally; and among those painted were many expressions besides hostility: dismay, confusion, confoundment, uncertainty. It gave me hope.

"Yes, Ira," Nyerza said, voicing my thoughts. "Doubt can be heartening—some of them do doubt. Doubt is the gate that opens to a long road—finally to truth."

"Shith on themth, fugemall," said the Bugsy. It gestured to three men near him who raised their rifles. "Killumbathuds!"

Nyerza opened his mouth to speak for peace—but a rattling, an echoing crackle of automatic fire erupted from the Guardsmen...

And the three mob riflemen fell dead.

The crowd fell back—backing away but not dispersing. An electric uncertainty holding them—holding us all—in place.

I tried to pull Melissa to cover but she gently pushed my hands away and fell to her knees, facing the mob, her lips moving in prayer. The holy men with us followed suit; each of them praying in the posture of his tradition.

There was a single gunshot from the mob, which whistled over our heads—a rifle shot from a shaking, skinny young man, naked and gaping. His tentative gunfire was returned by the Guardsmen—returned conclusively. He spun around with the impact of a dozen bullets, yelping once, and fell. The crowd cried out and drew back further, away from the fallen man; most of them throwing themselves down for cover or hunkering behind trees...A few dropped their guns and raised their hands.

Others took up shooting positions behind the trees.

The demons in the sky veered closer. The Bugsys raised their fists...

The Guardsmen took aim; the gunmen in the mob took aim.

Then the sky grew dark.

There were no clouds. But in fearful silence, the sky darkened of itself. I looked at the sun—there was no eclipse. All the sky, instead, was eclipsed; not blackened, but darkened so that a deep twilight reigned.

Then the Gold in the Urn emerged from Melissa.

The Gold shimmered and sparked in the air just in front of her, as she continued to pray. The orb seemed to grow—to become thirty, forty feet across. And as it grew details became evident. I seemed to make out a swirl of faces within the light, men and women of all races: ancient races and modern, Asian and European and African and Latin. Was that Mendel? It seemed so.

Everyone gazed at the Gold; it was the greatest source of light, with the sky blotted; even the Bugsys seemed frozen with a kind of profound misgiving, as they stared into the swirling radiance of sheer Conscious Being.

Melissa's voice came from somewhere—from the Gold as much as from Melissa—and it seemed to carry that more-than-human resonance that vibrated in the heart and the head as well as the ears: **"There are those held captive here only by their fear, and their uncertainty: to those I say, pray for self knowledge, pray to see yourself as you are, pray to see your connectedness to the Higher, and to see the false for what it is. Pray to see your rootedness in the nature-mind, in a self that is no individual but which delights in your individuality; pray to see your essence; pray to see your sleep; pray to ask for awakening. Pray for the murderers and the murdered. Pray for That Certain One; pray for demons and the demon-ridden; pray for your enemies; pray again for yourself. If you know that you know nothing, your prayers to know will be answered. Pray to see yourself as you really are..."**

There was an immediate response from many in the mob of demon-followers—a cry of despair paradoxically mingled with sudden hope. I saw almost half of them go to their knees. Praying—in the vocabulary of many spiritual traditions; praying to see themselves as they really were, the bad with the good. I saw their anguish, their relief. I heard them shouting—shouting many things, but all the same. I heard Shephard crying out, sobbing. I saw the Bugsys jumping up and down with fury…I saw Gnashers coming through the crowd from the rear, rending as they came…Then stopping, freezing in place, to make ready for what came next.

Then I saw the incubus. That's what I call it, anyway.

It didn't come all at once. The incubus seemed to come, at first, in questing fingers of iridescent-black ooze, that streamed across the gray dirt, between the dead trees, from a gathering of demons behind the mob; the demons seemed frozen in place like statues as the ooze nosed its way in rivulets and shiny-black glutinous branchings from them, to merge into a great pool before us—before the Gold in the Urn.

Like a sentient pool of petroleum the black syrup purposefully churned and took shape: many shapes, seven shapes.

Seven black imps stood before us, formed out of the pool—I stared at them, expecting to see a shape that corresponded to the Seven Clans. But they were all of the same shape, a silhouette of a human being, an androgynous human being, both male and female, each about two feet tall. They were all of inky liquid within, black but tinged with red; each was filmed over with an iridescent sheen that was almost exactly like the brackish colors gasoline makes on a puddle.

The imps rushed toward one another, and then bounded into a manic, circular dance, as we stared in disgusted wonder. The circle grew smaller, and they began to clamber, to cluster, to crawl stickily onto one another, like a sickening mockery of acrobats who make a tower of human bodies. They stood one atop the other, clutched together, and formed a shape synthesized from the sum of their small bodies, an almost Escherian formation of the big out of the small: a seven-foot-high incubus made of oily, iridescent, faceless imps, tightly clasped one against another. Its own face was just a crudely-thumbed suggestion of eyes and nose and mouth; a contemptuously-unfinished sketch. The imps that constituted its body seemed to squirm through its whole form, writhing up and down, their outlines visible within the androgynous shape of the incubus.

It turned its eyeless face toward our deputation, and we felt its gaze on us like a swarm of lice.

One of the holy men screamed and threw himself flat. With a hoarse cry Mimbala tried to rush at the thing—Nyerza pulled him back, but not before Mimbala fired a pistol at it, and we could see the vitreous-onyx surface ripple with the impact: but the bullet was drawn into it and swallowed, and forgotten.

But still Melissa knelt, praying; serene. Still the Gold in the Urn burned and turned in the air, unperturbed. The holy men prayed; Paymenz prayed; Nyerza prayed; and I...

I'm ashamed to record that I only stared at the scene in paralyzed fear.

The incubus reflected a little of the light of the Gold in the Urn, like the mirroring of a star in a pool of dirty water and gasoline. It took a step toward the Gold and put out its hands and the Gold reacted with a spasm that was a kind of retreat—revulsion acted out in pure light. Melissa only twitched; her face showed a sickened grimace; and then became serene again.

The demons howled in glee...

The incubus made to advance once more.

Then Shephard was up, staggering from his wheelchair, past the orb of light, directly into the path of the incubus. He shouted wordless defiance and flung himself at it, fists raised—and vanished shrieking into it as wholly and completely as the bullet had.

A useless sacrifice, I thought, choking with a grief that Shephard perhaps didn't merit—but then, for me, Shephard was all wretches who wanted redemption...And my grief for him was very personal...

Melissa stood and said, smiling, her voice calm and clear: **"He's there still—our lost friend Professor Shephard! All of you, here! Pray for this man who betrayed us all—pray for him!"**

The incubus seemed to hesitate at the edge of the circle of light—and took a step back. The light expanded to encompass the space the incubus had occupied...

The demons raged and stamped forward in desperation at this—but the light of the Gold, expanding warningly, held them at bay.

And we prayed for Shephard—who had vanished within the Incubus of the Seven Imps...

That was the incubus' undoing; a prayer for another, for an enemy, predicated on prayer for self knowledge...

So it seemed inexorably right when we saw Shephard's face—emerging from the Incubus—gone!—and then reappearing for a moment, one of the half-seen faces in the Gold in the Urn, weeping with joy.

And as Shephard appeared the Incubus began to fall apart—first into its component imps, then into a pool of black that seeped into the cracks of the Earth, and was gone from sight...

The demons roared in frustrated fury, but fell back before us as we followed the Gold in the Urn, and Melissa; as we marched forward, through the gate, and into the final Industrial Sacrifice Zone. And down into the underground, where more than a thousand slept in their own concrete, fluorescent-lit purgatory.

Those among the mob who had heard Melissa, who had prayed for self-knowledge, followed us joyfully through the gate, and into the underground place. And out again after it was over, back to what remained of their lives.

The demons lit into their remaining followers, rending in fury—but many paraders escaped, as the awakenings began, and the demons ran in terrified confusion…and began to fall away into themselves, falling into nowhere …Vanishing from the Earth…

Getting smaller with distance as they went nowhere at all.

*   *

Almost a year since I wrote the above.

The Gold in the Urn passed from Melissa, that day, months ago, as soon as she emerged from the final ISZ. She collapsed—but only from exhaustion.

She opened her eyes, once, as I wheeled her on a gurney to the plane. She murmured, "All sparks are struck… from…" Her eyes closed.

She was asleep—the good sleep—before she finished saying it. I said the rest for her: "…from the same forge."

She slept that good sleep for two days. When she woke, the Gold was gone, but she was forever changed. She awoke…*awake.*

Melissa is two months pregnant. I'm hoping for a boy. She's hoping for a girl. We argue about the name. Right now I'm in our bedroom, working at a little wooden "tv tray". I'm looking forward to us moving out of here, soon, and into our own place, something larger. Just now she's teaching a seminar at the Hall of Remembering; I'm supposed to meet her for dinner. Chinese food.

We're living with her father, who's had not only his electricity returned, and water, but has had an unspeakably large government grant quietly bestowed on him. "Perhaps," Paymenz chuckled, "the grant will go the way of this administration, if this rhetoric continues…"

He said this the night we watched with real amazement as, on the evening news, the government gave its official opinion that the demons had not existed as a physical reality, that it had all been some kind of hallucinogen-gas attack by a cult of industrialists who'd had an obscure world-domination plan. There was, somehow, no existing film footage of the demons; not on video, celluloid or digital. Nothing. It has all gone black. We have our own explanations for that; the officials have theirs. It doesn't matter.

All the deaths, the spokesmen say, were carried out by human beings, some of them in costume. Possibly some robotically augmented. Those who remember otherwise, say the spokesmen, remember hallucinations formed by suggestion, spawned by faked video and mass hypnosis. The prior President was supposedly killed by a hallucinogen-addled assassin.

The world tries to forget, as of course it must. A World's Fair is planned; an Olympics. There is much reconstruction. But there are enough of us who remember —millions who remember, who are sure of what they remember—and who know that the spiritual world is the material world; that the material world is the spiritual world; that the universe is just a conception in a mind that dreams what it must, that calls for us to return to its deepest places, through awakening to who we really are.

Me, I'm doing a little writing, and some graphics, for *Memorial Magazine,* which Paymenz funds and which I oversee. Melissa is just Melissa—most of the time. She only rarely chooses to show her true self to me. Her higher self is hard for me to look at—there are no sunglasses for that light. But she opens the shutters a little when she teaches the hundreds who come to her, to hear her speak at the unprepossessing little edifice they have built for her, the Hall of

Remembering, in an oak grove, on a former cattle ranch near Martinez.

And a sadly smiling, mustachio'd little man named Yanan has come from Turkey, to live near us. He was sent by Nyerza, he said, to be my special instructor, to prepare me for the time, maybe soon, maybe years from now, when I will enter the Conscious Circle.

Every so often, I take a step closer to that entrance, that place where I see myself as I really am; where I see *who* I really am; where I forgive the unforgivable. Every step toward that place is joyful—but every step hurts.